The fat man said he knew where the girl was

Simon Kaye had to find the girl. She knew all the answers. But he'd been an investigator for a long time. He smelled a trap. He followed the fat man anyway. And was led to a sagging apartment building in a downtown slum.

"She's in there," wheezed the fat man, pointing to a door. Kaye knew what was supposed to happen. He would walk right through that door—and die. Someone was waiting in the room for him—but it wouldn't be the girl.

He kicked the door open. Grabbed his fat guide. And threw him headfirst into the room. There was a scream. A hail of bullets. And then silence.

Dead silence.

D1513409

Keeping you in suspense is our business

RAVEN HOUSE takes pride in having its name added to the select list of prestigious publishers that have brought—in the nearly one and one-half centuries since the appearance of the first detective story—the finest examples of this exciting literary form to millions of readers around the world.

Edgar Allan Poe's *The Murders in the Rue Morgue* started it all in 1841. We at RAVEN HOUSE are proud to continue the tradition.

Raven House Mysteries

Let us keep you in suspense.

THE GLENNA POWERS CASE

Hillary Waugh

A RAVEN HOUSE MYSTERY FROM
WORLDWIDE
TORONTO · LONDON · NEW YORK

Raven House edition published February 1981
First printing September 1980

ISBN 0-373-60026-7

Printed in Canada

1

FATHER JACK MCGUIRE is a better priest than he is a chess player—at least I hope he is because I can beat him in chess and I'm not that good.

Except tonight he had me a piece down and he was enjoying it. We were in his study in the rectory sipping nonsacramental wine with a floor lamp over the board for light. I'm a heathen, but he lets me into his inner sanctum for three reasons: I play chess, he really doesn't believe I'm a heathen, and we grew up together. He gave me my first black eye and I gave him his first bloody nose. That was when we were six and he was new on the block. We've battled since then, but never with fists. We hit too hard.

"Hurry up and move," I said. "I can't stand seeing people gloat."

He rubbed his hands and said, "You think if you hurry me, I'll blunder?"

There came the distant sound of the door chime. It was ten-thirty on a November Sunday evening, and the house had been silent for hours. I looked up, but Jack didn't flicker an eyelash. He thought he had a mating combination.

Then Mrs. Honeywell, his housekeeper, came in from the

dark hall. Father McGuire had a visitor, a very distraught young woman. She was waiting in the parlor.

Jack nodded and got up, still with his eyes on the board. He studied it a moment longer while he buttoned his collar and put on his black coat, then he excused himself.

While he was gone, I pondered the board myself. Then I poured and sipped some more of his wine—damned good stuff. Jack knows his vintages and his vineyards. After that there was nothing to do but wander around looking at the books on his shelves. They're all about the Church and God and Christ and Christianity, which aren't my fare. I don't believe in God, let alone the rest of it.

I had twenty minutes like that before Jack returned. I was by his desk where I could see him coming down the hall with the light at his back, and I knew before I saw his face that he had troubles.

He entered the room and paused by his chair, smiling sadly.

"You've got a problem," I said, "and I should leave."

He shook his head. "I don't have the problem," he answered, "the young lady has the problem. And as a matter of fact, I'd rather you didn't leave. I think I could use your help, if you're willing to assist and can keep a confidence."

"Of course. What do you want done?"

He raised a hand and smiled. "You shouldn't be so quick, Simon. You haven't heard the problem yet."

"It doesn't matter."

"It might. There's a question of legality involved. If we got caught you could have your license suspended."

"What about 'Parish Priest Goes to Jail'? That wouldn't look so good on your record."

"Yes, but this is my business. However, judge for yourself." He led me down to the front parlor, which was the only other lighted room in the house.

The young woman Mrs. Honeywell had admitted was sitting on the edge of the couch. She was about twenty-eight years old, dark haired with a round face, short nose, full lips—an attractive but distressed face. She wore a blue dress and black pumps. She had good legs and a figure that was maybe five pounds too heavy. The black purse she carried was a little small for what she wanted it to hold and she clutched it in a death grip on her knees.

Jack introduced us. He told her I was Simon Kaye, a detective but not a police detective, and he told me her name was Glenna Powers. I said, "Father McGuire thinks I can help you."

She nodded. "Yes," she said softly, staring at me with dark, stricken eyes. "You see, I've just killed a man."

Jack interrupted. "Miss Powers, please. I didn't intend for you to tell him that."

"It's all right," she said. "He's got to know soon enough. It's not going to be a secret."

I stood and waited and I knew damned well that whatever she and Jack had cooked up was illegal. Maybe a priest can keep a confession like that in confidence, but the moment he does anything more than just listen he's going to make himself an accessory after the fact—and me along with it.

Jack said. "All right, I think Mr. Kaye had better hear all of it."

She looked up at me, gripping the purse as if it was a life preserver. "It's, ah, my sister," she said. "She's much younger. Only twenty." Glenna Powers's eyes kept going from me to the priest. "I raised her...after my folks died. Twelve years. She's kind of wild. She got in with the wrong people. Recently she's become involved with a very bad man. He got her on drugs."

She looked down at her purse. "I tried to keep them apart, but I couldn't. Today she left me and moved in with him. I found the note when I came home from helping a friend redecorate her room—maybe an hour ago." She looked up at me. "I didn't know what to do. I took a gun and went to his apartment. She was with him. She was...on drugs...spaced out. I couldn't stand it. I told him to let her go. I threatened to kill him if he didn't stop seeing her. But he only laughed at me. And—I didn't know what I was doing. I shot him." She looked at me beseechingly.

I eyed Jack. I couldn't figure it. Why wasn't she telling this story to the police? What did she want from a priest?

Jack said to her, "Tell him what you did after that."

She nodded obediently. "After I killed him—I...I was going to call the police. But my sister...I didn't want them to find her there. I wanted to keep her name out of this. She's only twenty. She could be ruined."

The girl shook her head slowly. "But she was...so doped up. I couldn't do anything with her." She breathed heavily for a moment. "I didn't know what to do. So I came to Father McGuire here. I thought he might help me—come with me to take care of my sister—or might know somebody...."

Jack said to me, "Now you see what I mean? If we get her sister out of there before Miss Powers notifies the police, we might be indulging in an illegal activity. I'm not that much up on the law myself, but I have a suspicion that the authorities would take a dim view of such an action."

I said to the girl, "Where is your sister and this man?"

She gave me a Stabler Street address. It was only a couple of blocks away, an apartment building on one of the bad streets in town. They're all bad in Jack McGuire's parish. The neighborhood wasn't good when we were growing up in it, and it's worse now. But even on the worst streets gunshots are going to attract attention.

I said, "How many times did you shoot him?"

"I don't really remember. Three, I think. I didn't know what I was doing."

"And after the man was dead, you spent some time trying to get your sister to leave with you, but she wouldn't?"

She nodded.

"What about the neighbors? Weren't they out in the hall wanting to know what happened?"

She again gave a negative shake of her head. "I don't think anybody heard it. It didn't make much noise. I didn't see anybody."

"Let me see the gun."

She said, "I don't have it. I left it there."

"With your sister stupefied on drugs? Her, a gun and a dead man?"

Glenna Powers looked ready to cry. "I was upset. I wasn't thinking. I never killed a man before."

I said to Jack, "We'd better get the hell over there fast."

We rode over in Glenna's car, a big rattletrap convertible with a rotting roof, which she'd inherited from her parents. It was after eleven now and the street was dark and dirty. The apartment building was on the corner of Vesey; an old building, but solid. When Jack and I were kids there used to be bushes around it and even a little grass, but now it was pavement.

The street in front was lined with cars, but there was space around the corner where Glenna had left hers before. We locked up and headed for the front door, and the night was quiet but sinister. There was no traffic, no people walking their dogs or coming back from the neighborhood movie. You didn't stay out after dark in this part of town, and the only sound was the wailing of a starving cat.

It was a seven-floor building and we rode a graffiti-riddled elevator to the sixth, Glenna standing between us with her head bowed. We got out and she walked us around the corner to 6F. The halls were empty, the silence was oppressive. It didn't seem real. In this building gunshots didn't turn people out? They kept behind their locked doors and didn't even call the police?

Glenna opened her purse in front of the door and fitted a key in the lock. I said, "Where'd that come from?"

She answered without missing a beat, "It was on the mantel. I took it when I left—to make sure I could get back in."

She opened the door and pushed it wide before entering. All the lights were on but nobody was in sight. She exhaled and entered, Jack and I followed. The door had four kinds of locks on it—it was that kind of neighborhood—and I engaged two of them so we wouldn't be disturbed. Ahead of us was a long, narrow living room-dinette combination with windows to the back-alley fire escape at the other end. A fake fireplace with an electric log was on the left, and the first thing Glenna did was replace the key on the mantel.

It was hard to see the dead man at first. He was behind the end of the couch, which faced the fireplace. There was a doorway there, separating the dinette section, and he was lying in it so that only his shiny bright shoes and the cuffs of his expensive trousers were visible.

I went first. This was my business rather than Jack's.

The man was dark haired and swarthy, with a face only a gold digger could love. His clothes were as expensive and soft as his eyes were cheap and hard. The eyes were black and wide, and they glittered in the light.

He'd got some blood on that expensive Brooks Brothers shirt. Some blood and some bullet holes. I counted three in a little triangle where whatever heart he had was supposed to be. There wasn't a lot of blood—at least not showing on the outside—and the three holes were loud and clear. They weren't small holes, either. They hadn't been made by popguns. You don't put holes like that into people without making a lot of noise about it.

The shirt was yellow flannel and buttoned at the throat, but there was no tie. The jacket was a spotty her-ringbone—grays and tans against an off-white backing with here and there a fleck of bright orange. The trousers were a soft light gray and must have felt good against the skin. His hair was marcelled, he wore rings on four fingers and he carried an empty gun holster on his belt. It was shaped to hold a .32 snub-nosed Colt.

Father Jack, as I sometimes call him, came up and stood beside me. Glenna hung back. She didn't like the look of dead bodies. I wouldn't have liked the looks of this one when it was alive.

I beckoned to her. "Where's the gun you say you shot him with?" It was obvious from the holes that he'd been plugged with something bigger than a .32.

"I hid it under the couch cushions."

She lifted them and it was still there. She handed it to me and I could believe it. It was a .38 long, fitted with a silencer. That could make three holes in the Brooks Brothers shirt and do it without rousing the neighborhood. No wonder the police hadn't been called. No wonder people hadn't opened their doors. Those three bullets would have sounded like three loud thumps and while they might have been heard in the outside hall, they wouldn't have been heard in the adjoining apartments.

"Very nice," I said, sniffing the gun, opening it and finding three spent shells.

I was still holding it when out from the bedrooms opposite a girl appeared. She was dark and attractive, like Glenna, but younger, more hellish, and she was completely nude. She came into the doorway and looked at the three of us and giggled.

Jack turned red. Naked damsels were not his scene and he didn't know what to do with his eyes. After the head-on view they went around her and around the room, fixing momentarily on the window curtains as if he could wrap her up in them if she'd be willing to stay wrapped.

Glenna stared, but without surprise, which told me that that was how she'd left her sister and was one of the reasons she'd gone for help. The kid sister didn't look anxious to get into her clothes and there'd be no way to force her. She was stoned to the eyeballs.

"Hello," the kid sister said and came into the room. She giggled again—at the way Jack looked everywhere except at her. She came closer and said teasingly, "Do you want to spank me, Father?"

I didn't look at Glenna. I didn't have to. I chucked the gun on the couch and took the kid by the arms and marched her back into her bedroom. The lights were on and her clothes were thrown across her suitcase. "Okay," I said. "You've had a lot of fun. Now get dressed."

"Make me."

Her pupils were pinpoints. She didn't know where she was and what she was doing. I slapped her across the face, hard. "You hear me?"

It didn't have the right effect. She sobered and shook her head and the grin came out again. "You're strong! I like you." She put her arms around me. I pushed her onto the bed and she didn't try to get up. She lay there invitingly, except she didn't know she was inviting. It just felt good to lie down.

I sorted through the clothes on the suitcase and threw her pants at her. "Put those on." I found her bra but didn't bother with that. The dress looked complicated, too. She'd never master that one, even with help. I looked at her. The pants lay across her stomach and she watched me. She hadn't moved. I picked them up and tried to get them over one of her feet. She started kicking.

I gave that up, threw them back on the suitcase and started for the door. I didn't get through it before she leaped on me from behind. I got pulled halfway around and her arms encircled my neck. "Kiss me," she breathed, "I love you, I love you."

That was great. Jack was staring, Glenna was staring, and this naked, nubile child was hanging on me as if I was a skyhook and she didn't have a parachute.

It took me a while to get free. I didn't want to hit her again—not in front of Glenna. Besides, I was afraid it would make her even more amorous. She seemed to go for the macho types. So we wrestled and I finally got loose, but

I had to hold her by both wrists. The thing was, she didn't know where she was at. She was really gone.

"Glenna," I said, "will you get her into the bedroom and sit on her?"

Glenna came quickly and talked soothingly, trying to make her listen. She put her arms around her and kept saying, "Come on, Chelsea, come with me, baby, it'll be all right," and gradually the kid's arms relaxed and I was able to let go.

Glenna coaxed her into the bedroom and I said to Jack, "This is the last time I ever play chess with you!"

He didn't laugh. He was more concerned than I. There was a dead man at his feet. There was a gun with a silencer on it lying on the couch. The girl who had confessed to the murder was in the bedroom calming a sister who wasn't wearing any clothes. This was not his usual kind of parish problem.

I went through the dinette, around a tea table and pair of chairs, and tested the windows to the fire escape. They formed a set of three and the middle one was unlocked. I threw it open, examined the sash and sill, leaned out and studied the fire escape—the steps up and the steps down. It made me look very businesslike—the big-shot detective doing his thing—but there wasn't anything to see.

When I came back in and shut the window, Jack was beside me, watching my every move, and Glenna was returning from the bedroom. I said, "Is sister getting dressed?"

Glenna shook her head. "I've got her sitting down, but that's all."

"That's not enough. We've got to get her out of here."

"I know."

"Was that the way you found her?"

Glenna nodded.

"And you couldn't get her to dress, and you couldn't take her out of here that way—"

Glenna turned and looked helplessly at Jack. "So I went to Father McGuire," she said softly.

Father McGuire tested me for answers. "What's your view, Simon?" he asked, wanting to see if I had anything he could buy. This was, after all, his neck. Even if it weren't, he has a very strict code of ethics and he wouldn't do anything that wasn't kosher—if an atheistic ex-Protestant can apply a Jewish term to a Catholic priest.

"I'll tell you what I recommend," I told him. "We leave the gun where it is. We wrap the kid sister up in her coat, we pack her clothes in a shopping bag, we pick up her suitcase and the four of us walk out of here like we're going to an all-night movie. Once we're clear and have little sister and big sister back home where they belong, you get on the telephone and tell the police—anonymously, of course— that you wish to report a body. You give this address and apartment number and hang up. On second thought, I'd better make the call."

Jack said, worrying about me, "You might be risking your license."

"Yeah, but I think I can say it better."

Jack didn't have a suitable alternative so we played it that way. Glenna and I took on the hard job—that of getting little sister into the coat she'd worn. She thought we were playing a game and she kicked and squirmed and giggled. It took a while but we got her tucked in and sat on—meaning I sat on her while Glenna took her suitcase to the front door and gathered all her clothes into a bundle.

"Make sure you've got everything," I said. "We don't want the police finding any leftovers."

Glenna was efficient and when she was sure she'd left nothing behind, I stood Miss Muffet on her feet and told her we were going bye-bye. She decided the way to stay where she was was to go limp. I caught her under the armpits just before she hit the floor.

I dragged her out like that, while she sang a song, and I can tell you, if I'd been alone I'd have knocked her cold and taken her out with the fireman's carry.

Glenna leaned over her and tried to talk some sense into her, but it didn't do any good. Finally Jack and I put her arms around our shoulders and walked her out that way. She saw the body on the floor when we went by and said, "Oh, lookit him." She didn't seem to know who he was or what he was.

I told her to say goodbye to him and Glenna made sure the hall was empty before we ventured forth and took sweetheart down in the elevator.

Glenna drove us to their house, Jack in front with her and Miss Playful in back with me. She was feeling amorous again and tried to make love to me all the way home. Between keeping her coat from falling off and her hands where they belonged, I needed more arms than an octopus.

2

ONCE WE GOT HER in her own room, little sister conked out, and you can make of that what you want. We laid her on her bed, still in her coat, and she sighed and turned over and fell fast asleep like a seven-year-old child who's been playing all day.

Jack was supervising and once we had the kid down he spread a blanket over her. We turned off the lights but left the bedroom door open. Glenna said Chelsea was afraid of the dark. She didn't seem to be afraid of much else.

We powwowed in the living room. Glenna wanted to get us some Coke or Seven-Up, but I told her to sit. Now that we'd escaped from Durance Vile, or whatever the name of the apartment was, she was walking on wires. Jack wanted to hip-hip-hooray and say, "My God, we did it." The only question was, what had we done? We'd taken a nude, doped-up girl out of a dead man's apartment. And what was that for? What were we trying to prove? Glenna had her reasons, I had mine, but Jack was along for the ride. He didn't know what it was all about.

Neither did I, but it was time to find out.

I told Glenna to relax, but I had to interrupt her pacing and take her by the shoulders and park her on the couch. Jack was on the edge of an overstuffed chair opposite, and

I remained standing. First things first, I told Glenna, and the first thing was the name of the dead man who was supposed to have been her sister's lover.

"Scorwitch," she said. "Ralph Scorwitch."

"And he put your sister on drugs?"

"He got them for her, at least."

"And the love affair? Where'd that story come from?"

"Story?"

"That they're in love."

"Well, you saw her." Glenna was flushing bright red. "You saw how she was dressed...undressed."

"I saw how she reacted to his body—giggly—pointing a finger and saying, 'Lookit him!' That's supposed to be love?"

"She was drugged. She didn't know what she was doing."

"She was climbing all over me in the back seat coming home and she knew what she was doing then. She's not in love with him. She never was."

Glenna said stubbornly, "She left home today to go to him."

"I know. She left you a note. Where's the note?"

"I threw it away."

"Shall we hunt through the garbage for it? It oughtta still be there. Or did you burn it instead?"

Glenna compressed her lips and didn't answer. She darted a glance at Jack but he was saying nothing, looking nothing, just listening and absorbing.

I said, "What really happened at that apartment this evening?"

"I told you," she said stubbornly. "I went to bring Chelsea home. Ralph let me in. I found her like that. She wouldn't come with me, and he laughed at me when I threatened him with the gun. I shot him, but I couldn't leave her there, and she wouldn't come with me. So I—"

"So you went to Father McGuire and so on and so on. Where'd you get the gun you shot him with?"

"I bought it."

"Where?"

"From one of Chelsea's friends. I don't remember who."

"Why?"

"I thought I might need it to rescue her sometime."

"All right," I said, "now let's stop the lying. You didn't kill Ralph Scorwitch any more than I did—"

"But that's not true," she interrupted. "I did kill him. Why would I say I killed somebody if I didn't?"

"Because you're trying to shield your sister." I bent over her. "Now listen to me, don't you go confessing to the police, do you understand? Because they aren't any more gullible than I am. In two minutes they'll know you think your sister did it and that's what they'll believe. They won't believe *you* did it, but they'll damned well believe *she* did."

"But, but—" she protested. "How can you say such things? I ought to know what I did."

"You damned well *do* know what you did—and killing Ralph Scorwitch wasn't it. You don't know anything about guns and you don't know anything about silencers. A silencer on a gun is the mark of a killer who's done a lot of advance planning, not some girl who's going after the guy her sister ran off with that afternoon. You aren't packing a gun that size, with silencer included, in a purse like the one you're carrying. That purse hardly holds all the stuff you've crammed into it already. You're trying to take the rap because you're convinced that little sister in the back room there killed her own boyfriend. And that doesn't make a lot of sense, either. Now suppose you straighten up and tell Father McGuire and me what really happened. God wants you to—at least that's what Father McGuire tells me. And I want you to because if you don't, your sister's likely to be nailed as the killer, and if she is, you'd be the one who nailed her."

Glenna was looking at Jack now and she was frightened. "Father," she whispered, "what does he mean?"

If nothing else, Jack is succinct. "He's telling you to tell the truth," he said.

"Should I?"

"You should always tell the truth."

Glenna wasn't all that sure, but she was frightened enough not to put up a fight about it. "My sister didn't know what she was doing," she told me. "You saw her. You saw how she behaved."

I had vivid memories of how she behaved. She was a pain in the rear end, but she sure as hell was a sexy piece of pain. She could leave you lying awake at night. "I saw how she behaved," I said.

"She's harmless. She wouldn't hurt a flea."

"Spoken like a true mother. Now tell Father McGuire and me what happened."

She went through her paces again and this time it sounded a little better. She'd come home from her friend's, as she'd told us before. But there really hadn't been any note. What there had been was a missing suitcase and some empty bureau drawers. Glenna didn't need to be told what that meant. They'd quarreled about Ralph Scorwitch earlier and Glenna had tried the fruitless tactic of demanding that Chelsea never see him again.

Glenna drove to Scorwitch's place, went up to the apartment and was prepared to lay down the law to both Chelsea and Scorwitch, threatening them with whatever legal recourses she could invent.

Before she could knock, however, she heard three quick, strange popping sounds and a thud. That worried her. She thought something was being done to Chelsea and she started pounding on the door and calling. After a bit, it was Chelsea herself who opened it. She was as we had seen her, nude—and she was holding the gun and silencer in her hand. Glenna, in a panic, had rushed in and discovered Scorwitch lying as we'd discovered him. No one else was in the apartment and she assumed, naturally, that Chelsea, in her drugged state, had shot the man. Glenna's only thought was to get Chelsea away from there, but Chelsea was uncooperative and incapable. Realizing she couldn't remove Chelsea from the scene without help, she tried to protect the girl from the murder charge by assuming it herself and going to Father McGuire, hoping he would help shield her sister.

Well, fine. Glenna wasn't smart, she was protective. What wasn't smart was that she couldn't adequately explain where she'd acquired the gun and silencer. What also wasn't smart was her thinking that Chelsea could have acquired them.

I was teed off. Glenna was trying to pull off a con job that wouldn't fool a cigar-store Indian. These damned kids get themselves in a spot and think they can invent an explanation that's going to be swallowed by the pros. If Glenna hadn't come to us, if she'd gone to the cops instead, sister Chelsea would have been sitting—wrapped in a bathrobe from some lieutenant's locker, no doubt—in a jail cell at this moment.

I told Glenna she sure as hell was lucky. Now I wanted to phone the anonymous tip to the police.

The phone was on the table by the couch and Jack and Glenna listened while I talked. I got Sergeant Walker on the line. He knows me so I disguised my voice. "I want to report a murder," I said, and when he started the business about who was I and where did I live, I said my name and address didn't matter, what mattered was the name and address of the victim. I gave him those and said that he'd been shot three times by a .38 with silencer, that the front door was only snap-locked, and that it looked as if the killer had fled by the fire escape.

He tried to ask more questions, but I hung up and put the phone back on the table. Jack and Glenna were staring at me. Glenna said, "Is that to throw the police off the track?"

"Hell, no," I said. "I think that's how the killer did escape."

"But what about Chelsea?"

"The way she was doped up she couldn't have put three bullets in Scorwitch's chest if he'd stood still and let her. And where do you think she'd get a gun like that? That's professional artillery. It's my guess Scorwitch made the wrong enemies and that killing was the work of a hired assassin."

"But I heard the shots," Glenna said.

"That's right, and you started pounding on the door and the killer chucked the gun and went out the window. Then your sister comes into the living room to see what the racket's about, picks up the gun for want of anything dumber to do, and opens the door for you."

Jack said, "You think the assassin came in through the window, too?"

I shook my head. "My guess is he came through the door—that Scorwitch let him in, believing he was a buyer or dealer of something. From the barricades on that door it's a safe bet Scorwitch didn't leave his windows unlocked. And I gather from what Glenna says that little sister didn't have to do more than twist the knob to let her in. That would be because Scorwitch undid all the other locks when the killer came."

Glenna put her hands to her cheeks. "I can't get over it. You mean Chelsea didn't do anything?"

"She did a lot of things, but she didn't commit murder."

"Then we're free! I don't have to worry. I don't have to take the blame!"

I said, "I don't know if you're free or not. When the cops find a body, they start looking very hard at everybody who knew the victim. If Scorwitch has your sister's name in a little black book somewhere, or if he's mentioned her around town, she'll probably be in for a grilling."

That had Glenna chewing her lip again. I got up. "But don't worry about that till it happens. If it does, let me know. And one other thing: as soon as your sister knows what she's doing, I want you to have her call me. I want to find out what she remembers about tonight."

Jack and I took a cab back to the rectory, but we didn't return to the chess game. It was half-past one and I drove home to bed.

I WAS GOING OVER REPORTS on a missing person's case in the office next morning when Eileen came in with a ten-o'clock cup of coffee. She's my secretary and a dark-haired beauty who wears low-cut, very unsecretaryish dresses—which is good for business. What she doesn't reveal looks even more tempting than what she does, and that's good for business, too. It's only bad for business in one way because it hampers my concentration—a fact she gets a kick out of—but that problem is solved by keeping her in the outer office. She's not just looks, either. She slings a mean typewriter, takes shorthand faster than Gregg—but not on my lap—and has a memory that doesn't need file cabinets. She only keeps the files for knuckleheads like me.

Anyway, she put the coffee on my desk and said, "There's a young thing in the outer office looking for you." Eileen wrinkled her nose. "She says you're expecting her."

"Young thing?"

"Very young. Hardly weaned."

That meant old enough, and pretty besides. You have to know Eileen. She's twenty-three and anything below that age that doesn't have two heads is a threat.

I got to my feet. "Send her in, nurse, and stand by."

"Oh," she said. "One of those?"

She went out, and in a minute Chelsea came in. She was well brushed and combed, bright eyed and alert, looking as innocent and attractive as the sunrise. She wore clothes for a change: brown shoes, henna dress with buttons down the front, hat and bag. She wasn't wearing a bra, however, a fact that in her case became instantly obvious—and which accounted for Eileen's archness. Eileen pretends a lot of things, but she's a very moral girl. Which is a handicap against the Chelsea types.

"Here I am," Chelsea announced. "Glenna said you wanted to see me." She spun around in front of the desk to show off all her curves. "Or do you want to see me the way I was at Ralphie's?"

So she had a recollection of Ralphie's? That was promising. "You're showing off enough now," I told her. "Last night was overdoing it."

"You didn't think so at the time. You liked every minute of it."

"You remember a lot."

"I remember all the good parts."

I led her to the customer's chair and she liked the feel of my hand on her bare arm. She turned to me and tilted her face. "How about a kiss?"

"Do you remember me slapping you?"

She nodded and kept her pucker. "I loved it. Kiss me."

I pushed her and she fell into the chair. I sat on the edge of the desk. "Now let's talk some sense, Chelsea. Believe it or not, this is important. I want you to tell me everything you can remember about last night."

"I remember the back seat of the car. You had the hots for me."

"Do you think you can elevate your mind a little higher—say above the waist?"

"I'm not bad up there, either." She reached for the top button of her dress. "D'you want to see?"

I got off the desk. "I'm going to call in my secretary and you're going to dictate a statement to her explaining everything that took place yesterday. You're going to tell everything you know about the man who was murdered."

Chelsea stood up, too. "Oh, no," she said. "If that woman comes in here, I'm leaving. I'm not going to talk to her *or* to you."

"Maybe you'd rather talk to the police?"

"I'll talk to you, but not in front of her. I don't talk to men with women around."

I said, "You've got some interesting hang-ups, kid, but suit yourself. One way or another, you're going to have to talk."

"Only to you."

"All right, sit down and talk."

She grinned. "Why don't you knock me down? It gives me the hots."

Knock her down? I wanted to knock her cold. "I'll give you one more chance," I said. "Either you talk to me here and now, or I'll throw you to the wolves. Make up your mind."

She sat down at the threat and tried to pay attention. "What wolves?"

"You were in the apartment with a dead man last night. The police are going to want to talk to you about that. And when they talk to you, you're going to tell them things. You may not want to, but you will. You might not even know you're doing it, but you will. And if the things you tell them are bad, you're going to be in deep trouble. If they aren't bad, then you'll only be in shallow trouble. You may be able to get out of it."

She wasn't grinning now. She had turned pale. "I don't want to talk to the police," she said.

"Then talk to me. Tell me what you know and I might be able to help you."

"How?"

"I might be able to keep the police from knowing you were involved. I'm not saying I can, but I might. But that depends on what you tell me."

She shrugged a little, then sat back in the chair and half closed her eyes. "What do you want to know?"

"Start from the beginning. You packed a suitcase yesterday afternoon and walked out of the home you share with your sister. Why?"

"I hate my sister."

"Why?"

"She thinks she's my mother."

"Why?"

"Because she's older than I am and doesn't approve of my behavior."

"Why?"

Chelsea opened her eyes enough to glower at me. "Can't you say anything but why?"

"Why's a good word to get answers with. All right, you packed and left because you didn't like your sister. Why did you go to Ralph Scorwitch's place?"

"I didn't have any place else."

"So you knew he'd take you in. Why? What's your relationship to him? How did it start? How did it develop? Let's hear the story."

"It's not a very pretty story."

"I wasn't thinking of printing it in a Sunday-school journal. Let's hear it, warts and all."

She got on with it then and I don't know how much of what she said was true. Chelsea wasn't bothered by obstacles such as veracity, integrity and morality. She was a free soul. Maybe she was more a freewheeling soul. She'd met

Ralph Scorwitch three months before at a party. She didn't remember whose; she went to lots of parties. Yes, there was pot and other drugs.

Then he had a party; an orgy—meaning sex, drugs and booze—in a big building out of town. He rented it or knew the owners or something. It was a real blast—a three-day weekend party where anything went. Anything that Ralph Scorwitch was into turned out super. And he had more damned kinds of drugs! Anything you wanted, Ralphie-boy could get you. In the beginning it was gratis, but he couldn't hand out free samples forever so then you had to pay— about the time you decided you couldn't get along without the stuff.

Chelsea liked the drug scene, but she wasn't hooked— she didn't think she was. He wasn't really charging her. He was still feeding her a lot of freebies. It gave her the feeling she was special. And he was great for a good time—really great. And anytime he could do anything for her, all she had to do was call.

That was what she'd done the previous afternoon. Glenna was always ragging her, complaining, threatening her, trying to get her to come down out of the hallucinatory mists and become part of the real world. So she packed her things and tried to get Ralphie-boy, except he didn't answer the phone until midafternoon. She told him her problem and he said sure she could bunk in with him.

She hopped a bus with her big suitcase and he was waiting for her, unlocking his battery of locks to let her in. He had to go out, he told her, and parked her things in the spare bedroom and gave her a few joints to smoke and some of the harder stuff to help her pass the time. He went out and she got out of her things—she hated clothes—and besides, she had to be ready to do her duty by him and thought it would be easier to get the preparations out of the way before she got stoned. Thereafter she proceeded to entertain herself with the pills and smokes that good old Ralphie had left for her.

She told it like that to that point and then stopped.

"What happened after that?"

"I went to sleep."

"And when you woke up?"

"I was home in bed with a coat on and a blanket over me."

"You weren't alseep the whole time."

"If I wasn't, you can't prove it by me."

"What about the ride home in the back seat of the car? What about the slap I gave you?"

Her eyes widened. "Oh, yes. The back seat. I *do* remember that. Did I ever have the hots for you." She studied me thoughtfully. "And I still do. Right now. So it couldn't have been the drugs."

"You remember that. And you remember me slapping you. And you remember the dead man on the living-room floor. That was Ralph, wasn't it?"

"Dead man?" Her eyes had glazed.

"And the gun. Where did the gun come from?"

"What gun?"

I was losing my temper. "Listen, Miss Chelsea Powers, I told you—either you talk to me or you're going to talk to the police. Which is it?"

"But," she answered innocently, "if I have nothing to tell, what's there to talk about?"

I threatened her, I warned her, I even tried coaxing her. She liked all the approaches equally well. She wasn't hearing me, she was watching me. It was fun and games.

I finally threw her out of the place. She was useless.

3

THE AFTERNOON PAPERS carried the story with a small head-line on page two: "Stabler St. Resident Found Murdered." That said nothing at all and the story said little more. A man named Ralph Scorwitch had been brutally murdered in his apartment. He had been shot three times in the chest and was found, fully clothed, on the floor of his living room. His wallet and valuables had not been touched, there were no signs of burglary or forced entry. There was no known motive. The victim had been living at that address for nearly eight months. He had no known relatives in the area. Neighbors said he was quiet and minded his own business. Police said they were following a number of leads.

Well, it was none of my concern. At least so I thought.

Then, at three o'clock, I got a call from Glenna. The police had just come by the telephone company where she worked to ask where her sister was. It seems they'd found no one at home. She told them she had no idea, and she hadn't. That's what she was calling me about. Where could Chelsea have gone?

I said I didn't know, but there could be a couple of hundred easy answers: shopping, bridge with the girls, to the park to feed the pigeons—

"You know better than that!"

"How about a bar, an opium den, a massage parlor?"

"Stop it. I'm worried. Did she come see you?"

I told her she had and that I'd pitched her out on her ear. (It wasn't on her ear that I'd actually pitched her.) "I warned her either she talked to me or she'd be talking to the police. Maybe she's hiding because she believes me."

"Mr. Kaye, would you find her for me?"

"Me go look for her? I'd rather spearfish for piranha."

"I'm worried, Mr. Kaye. I'm sure something's happened to her. I'm afraid I don't have much money, but I could pay you in installments, couldn't I?"

I felt like telling Glenna she was going to spend her life worrying about her sister, but that's what she was already doing and it would never stop—not as long as Chelsea was alive. And I had a feeling Chelsea wasn't cut out for longevity. She didn't act the part. But Glenna wasn't the type to be dissuaded.

Chelsea was lucky at that. There was someone in the world to look after her, since she didn't look after herself.

"All right," I sighed, then pulled over a pad and quizzed Glenna on all the material I like to have about a missing person if I'm going to try to find him—the vital statistics, the habits, the hates and fears, loves and hopes, the dreams and the nightmares. When I was satisfied, I told her to sit back and relax and I'd be in touch.

The first thing I did was call Father McGuire. He was at home, which was usually not the case, and I said, "What are you doing, planning your next chess move?"

"You mean you aren't calling up to resign?" Then he told me he was working on his sermon for next Sunday. "I'm trying to find a moral in what happened last night, but I think I'm going to have to wait awhile. By the way, exactly what *did* happen last night?"

I said, "That's what I'm trying to find out." Then I told him about the kid sister, her behavior that morning, the fact the cops were after her, that she had disappeared and big sister wanted me to find her. "She hasn't come your way by any chance, has she?"

Father McGuire hadn't seen her and said he wasn't surprised. "While Glenna turns to priests when she's in trouble, I don't think Chelsea has the same inclinations."

"No," I said. "She heads for the Ralph Scorwitches of the world—with results such as you saw last night."

I thought next of checking with the police but decided that wouldn't be very smart. If they'd caught her, we'd find out soon enough. If they hadn't, they'd be breathing down my neck because I was interested.

I put Eileen on hold instead and took the car out to where Glenna and Chelsea lived. They'd inherited a single-family house on a fifty-by-a-hundred-and-fifty-foot lot in among numberless other single- and double-family dwellings lining both sides of the street for blocks and blocks in all directions.

It was three-thirty and Glenna wouldn't be home for two hours, but I wanted to see the place without waiting and I figured it wouldn't be hard to get into. Three cars were parked on the street, which is about the normal expectancy. Most people put their cars in the backyard but there are always the exceptions, or the visitors or relatives who drop in. That would explain two of the cars, but it didn't explain the small black Lincoln, six doors away on the opposite side of the street. What made that vehicle unique was that a man was in it, studying something in his lap that could have been a map or a book. He wasn't doing anything or being anything, he was only there, and that was what made him unusual. People don't customarily spend time sitting in parked cars. So I noticed him only because I notice anything unusual. There could be twenty different reasons for him to be sitting in his car, eighteen of them innocent. On the other hand, he might have been trying to steal the car or he might have been watching the house I was going to break into or something like that.

I gave him a look as I went by, and he looked up at me. He was a swarthy man with a hard face and brittle eyes and I both noted his license number and decided against making a frontal assault on the Powers girls' home. He didn't look as if he belonged in the neighborhood any more than I did.

The game I played was to park in front of the house beyond, get out, slam the door and walk along the driveway to the back, making like a long-entrenched resident. The rear yard was empty so I crossed over, jumped a small flower bed that marked the boundary, and mounted the porch of the Powers's house.

The back door had a snap lock and I was able to get through without trouble. The inner door required a skeleton key, and then I was inside. I went first to the living room, where the front windows gave a view of the Lincoln down the street. It and the driver were still there.

I went through the house after that, room by room and quickly. For that kind of work you don't probe toilet tanks and look at the undersides of all the furniture. It was enough to check the closets and drawers, try to determine whether clothes and suitcases were gone, and if so, what kinds. You also look to see if timetables have been left around, or if items or ads in newspapers have been marked.

You see what's in the wastebaskets, what's been written on the telephone pads, what is or isn't in the sugar bowl, that sort of thing.

There was nothing to find, which indicated to me that Chelsea hadn't gone far and wasn't planning to stay long. The day before she'd moved out with a suitcase full of clothes. Today the suitcase was in her closet and the clothes were back in her drawers. If she'd gone away, she didn't have another Ralph Scorwitch to move in with.

Nor did she have any money. Glenna had assured me of that when she called. Chelsea might be carrying a few dollars in her purse, but that was it. Glenna was sparing with what she doled out to her sister.

I was done in little over twenty minutes and took another look out the front window. The black Lincoln was gone and my guess that the guy might be watching this house appeared wrong. I'm wrong about a lot of things.

I left via the back way again, locking the doors as I'd found them, and walked out the same driveway I'd come in by. It didn't matter that the guy in the Lincoln was no longer watching. Somebody else might have been. When you fake something, you fake it all the way.

I spent the rest of the afternoon back at the office clearing up the routine stuff. At six I headed home for supper and another go at the chase-Chelsea strategy. Glenna didn't know any of Chelsea's friends other than Ralphie-boy and I hadn't found any handy-dandy address books that would let me track her down by ringing door-bells. Other tactics were needed.

I slid my heap into the marked slot that goes with my condominium and went up the steps. I have a sheltered entry that faces away from the neighbors, making it hard for them to see who comes and goes. The condominium complex is designed like that, to give maximum privacy in minimum living space.

I opened the door to the enclosed stoop and there, sitting on the sill of my front door, looking very impatient with it all, was Chelsea Powers.

"Christ," she said, getting to her feet. "I thought you'd died."

"Don't you have a home?" I asked her, unlocking the door. "Do you know your sister's hired me to find you, the cops are beating the bushes and the marines are about to land?"

"I don't like my home," she said, entering and spinning around in my foyer. "I like it here, though. Nice shag carpet, neat, tidy surroundings. Very livable."

"The cops picked up your name," I told her, trying to get the impact across.

She wandered through the apartment, turning on lights; the dining area, the sunken living room with a view of the woods, the kitchen with a view of the approach road and the condominium across the way, then up the carpeted stairs to the two bedrooms and bath. She had no trouble determining which was the master and which was the guest bedroom. The master is larger, faces the woodlands, is masculine and has a lived-in look. She studied my cabinet headboard with the clock radio, the TV controls, the bookshelves and books, the reading lamps, and she noted the king-size bed and the monogrammed coverlet. "Umm," she said. "Bedrooms are for living." Then she started unbuttoning her dress.

During this unguided tour I tried to explain to her that, like it or not, she was going to have to talk to the police; that there was no point in attempting to hide out; that interrogation wasn't all that bad, and I'd go through it with her if she didn't want a lawyer or was afraid to go it alone. When she got unbuttoned to the waist I had to concede we were playing her game, not mine, and I took hold of her wrists. "Yoo-hoo. Do you talk English? This is not the locker room of the Y.W.C.A."

She looked up at me with singular innocence. "Would you believe that I never thought it was?"

"Good. Then button up, because I'm taking you home to your sister."

"Really," she said, straining but not struggling against my grip, "I'm not all that bad. If you'd allow me to take off my dress, I think you'd find that I'm not bad at all."

"I found that out last night," I told her. "You're great. In fact, you're sensational. You don't have to prove it again tonight."

She got bitter at that. She didn't like the thought that the body beautiful couldn't buy all the goods in the store. "What the hell is it with you?" she snapped angrily. "Don't you like women? No, that's not the answer. I found out better. You lech for me, you bastard, but you won't take me. What is it, some goddamned puritanical upbringing's got you tied up in knots?"

I sat her down beside me on the bed. She had relaxed a little and I released her wrists and did up her buttons. She wasn't wearing a bra, as I've said before, and all she had on under her dress were her pants. I talked to her while I did her up and I made it short and sweet. "No," I told her, "I'm not puritan, and yes, you are a sexy morsel, and if things were right I'd be unbuttoning instead of buttoning and you wouldn't get out of here until morning, and by then you'd hardly be able to stand, let alone walk.

"But things are not right—not for that sort of thing. Your sister has hired me to find you and bring you back and I have an obligation to do just that. And part of that obligation is that I don't tamper with the merchandise. I return you to your sister as good as I found you."

"That's a crock of—"

"It's very old-fashioned," I agreed. "It's hard to explain to the modern generation—"

"Modern? You can't be more than thirty."

"There's still a gap between us, and it's more than age and it's not something you'd understand and it's not something I'm going to try to explain. What I'm doing is telling you. I've been hired to do a job and I'm on the job and while I'm on the job I don't fool around."

"How much is my sister paying you to find me?" Chelsea asked suspiciously.

"I'm not going to charge her for more than gasoline— just something to make it official. I didn't have to do anything. I can't seem to un-find you."

"Well, if it's only a technicality, what the hell are you so prudish about? When I'm hot for a guy he's never going to forget me—especially if I'm not doped up." She tried to unbutton her dress again.

It was wearisome. I pulled her hands away. "Now be a nice, grown-up girl. Learn to keep your clothes on." I stood up and raised her to her feet and took her downstairs where the motivations wouldn't be as strong. "You're going to be talking to the police," I said. "They're going to want a description of the man who killed your friend. Can you give a good description?"

"What's it worth to you?" She was being arch now, the pouty child who didn't get her way.

"Not me, Chelsea," I told her. "The police. You understand? The police! They want to know who killed Ralph. They want you to help them find out."

"I didn't see anything."

"I think you did."

"Why?"

"A lot of reasons—the length of time between the shots and your opening the door, the fact you were holding the gun in your hand. What'd he look like, Chelsea? You ever see him before?"

She looked through me.

"Forget it," I told her and went to the phone. "What's your number?"

She wouldn't even tell me that.

"You're a sweetheart," I said and opened the phone book.

She was snappish. "You don't do anything for me, I don't do anything for you."

"Up yours." I found the number and dialed it.

Chelsea came closer. "What're you going to do?"

"Tell your sister I've found you."

"Don't try to take me back to her because I'm not going. I'm twenty years old and I can do what I want."

"Only on this side of the law, baby. Only on this side of the law."

"Don't tell me."

Glenna picked up the phone and I explained to her who I was and what I had. Chelsea was, I announced, at this moment in my condominium, safe and sound but not manipulatable. "She says she's not going home to you."

"But she's all right?"

"As right as she usually is."

"Thank God. My mother and father—bless their souls—would never forgive me. Listen, I'll be right over. And how much do I owe you?"

"She says she won't go home with you."

"I know, but keep her there, all right? And how much do I owe you?"

"Nothing."

"But I must owe you something."

"Believe me, I didn't find her, she found me."

"But your time is valuable. You're keeping her till I get there—"

"Five dollars—so you can sleep at night. Any more and *I* wouldn't sleep at night."

"All right, I'll be right out. Where are you?"

I gave her the address and directions. "She says she's not going home with you," I reminded her one last time. "And don't forget, she's above the age of consent."

"I know," Glenna said, signing off. "I just want to talk to her."

I hung up and relayed that message to Chelsea. She made a face and uttered a foul word. I said, "She's your sister."

Chelsea had a few more foul words to go with the first one. It seems that older sister Glenna felt that the duties of both motherhood and fatherhood had fallen upon her shoulders when their parents died. Glenna was going to do the rearing job her folks hadn't lived long enough to accomplish. Chelsea, on the other hand, was going to see to it that she didn't.

So far Chelsea was winning.

WHILE WE WAITED for Glenna I tried to make some head-
way with Chelsea. She'd given me certain essentials that
morning, but I was probing new areas. It wasn't that I was
interested, because I wasn't. As soon as Glenna took
Chelsea off my hands I was rid of the whole business and I
didn't care whether I got my five bucks or not.

I had two goals in mind. The essential one was to keep
Chelsea occupied so that she wouldn't, for lack of anything
else to do, start undressing again. The other was that Police
Captain Perriod Marstan, who was a friend of mine, would
probably supervise the Ralph Scorwitch murder case and if
I could pick up a few tidbits for him it would be my
pleasure.

Primarily I was interested in prying out of Chelsea a
description of Ralph's murderer. She had to have seen him
and I wanted to know if the description fitted the guy
parked in the Lincoln down the block from the Powers's
home.

Chelsea was uncooperative. I was no longer her friend
and lover. I'd told her sister on her and that made me her
enemy. Now she was as stalwart as Hester Prynne display-
ing her "A" and I was one grade below mouse dung.

So she sat on a chair at the dining-room table and studied
the foyer through which Glenna would ultimately come. All
I could think, watching Chelsea's grim silence, was that it
was a good thing she didn't have a weapon. She really hated
her sister.

There was no use talking to her: she ignored me. That's
why she'd picked that chair — at the end of the dining table,
at the edge of the entrance hall. Her back was to everything

else and her mind was turned off. She'd make some guy a wife one day—if he didn't know what he was doing.

I played hard to get, which was easy. I sat in the sunken living room, with the curtains drawn against the windows and the multichanneled color TV on. Nothing can make the time go faster.

Chelsea stared at the backside of the front door and I stared at the TV screen, and as far as I could make out, both of us were equally well entertained.

Then came the sound of a car, up the slanting roadway from the central condominium area into our particular arm. It was Glenna; there was no mistaking the rattles of that catarrhal convertible. Chelsea tensed. Her reaction was something to see. She would do anything to avoid Glenna and the family homestead. She already had.

The car engine quit, the door slammed. Right outside the condominium.

There was the sound of Glenna's footsteps on the iron staircase to my storm-porch entrance, and I moved past Chelsea to let her in.

Then there were three strange thumping sounds and the footsteps stopped.

An interval of silence fell and I spent it pulling out my gun and running to the door. I yanked it open in time to hear the clatter of something heavy tumbling down the metal staircase.

It was Glenna.

And she was dead.

4

I SNAPPED OFF THE LIGHT so I wouldn't be a target, crouched and moved down a step so my gun could cover the area. Across the way, a car started up and shot off down the slope with its lights out. I got a look at it when it passed the arc lamp at the bottom: it matched the small black Lincoln that had been parked on Glenna's street.

I went down to Glenna then, to what was left of her. She lay at the foot of the stairs, near the front wheel of her convertible, her eyes staring at the stars, her mouth hanging slack. She wouldn't be worrying about Chelsea any longer. She wouldn't be worrying about anything any longer. She'd gone to a better world—at least I hoped it was better—but she hadn't been ready to leave this one. There was still too much she wanted to do.

I stood up and looked past the rear of the convertible down the slope after the vanished Lincoln, and I said aloud, "I don't know who the hell you are, but I'm going to find out and I'm going to kill you."

Standing there, feeling the way I did, I wished I'd snapped off a shot after that fleeing, spotless getaway car. There hadn't been time to take aim, but I might have put a bullet hole through the roof or one of the windows, might have left a mark I could trace it by. Now all I had was the plate number on the parked Lincoln and I couldn't swear that the two cars were the same. Why would a car that was staking out Glenna's place this afternoon be staking out my place tonight? Nobody knew I was involved. Nobody except Jack McGuire.

Chelsea appeared on the stoop above. She was clutching her dress around her throat, readying herself for something bad. "Simon? What is it?"

I went up the steps to her, two at a time. "Come back inside, Chelsea, we've gotta talk."

She pointed at the dark, sprawled heap at the foot. "What's that?"

"Inside."

"No. It's Glenna, isn't it? She's dead, isn't she?"

"Come inside. I want to talk to you."

She shook me off. One thing about Chelsea, she had a mind of her own. She switched the lights back on, and now she could see. "Glenna! Oh, my God."

I grabbed her and she struggled. I said, "You're not to go down there."

"It's my sister. Leave me alone. It's my sister."

She was getting violent and I let her go. Maybe it was better that way. She flew down and knelt by the silent spectral figure at the bottom. She shook her gently but knew it would do no good. Then she clasped her sister to her breast and kissed her face, uttering little incantations and complaints. She'd claimed she hated her sister, but you wouldn't know it now. Now, when it was too late, she was kissing her. Now she threatened to fall to pieces.

"Chelsea," I called to her softly. Lights were on in neighboring condominiums, but no doors had opened. It was like the previous night. The killings made no noise.

Chelsea looked up at me, still cradling her sister.

"You can't stay there. We've got to call the police."

"I know," she said, with remarkable control. "I'll be right there. I'm just saying goodbye."

I went inside, and Chelsea joined me a minute later. Her face was solemn, but not stricken. She'd made what peace with her world that she needed—not for all time, but for *that* time. "I'm all right," she said, but her eyes glittered. "Who did it, Simon?"

"If you could tell me who shot Ralph last night, maybe I could tell you who shot Glenna."

That ploy didn't work. "Now you know that's nonsense," she countered. "You were out there. You saw what happened. Who did it?"

"I don't know, and don't give me an argument." I took her by the shoulders. "Remember one thing in this. You and I are on the same side. We're going to get that sonuvabitch. Right?"

She nodded soberly. "Right."

"I'm going to report this to the police. But first, sit." I pushed her into a chair. "Because before I call the police I'm going to tell you a story and you're going to listen to it very carefully, and then you're going to do what I say. Understood?"

For once Chelsea was pliable. This didn't mean she was going to buy what I tried to sell, it only meant she would listen to the sales talk.

I made it short and sweet. I told her about the Lincoln with its swarthy driver that had been posted on her street that afternoon. I told her the same Lincoln had been posted outside of my apartment tonight. I said the driver had killed her sister. "Do you know who he is?"

Chelsea's eyes were veiled. "Why do you say he was staking out this place?" she asked. "Maybe he was following my sister."

I shook my head. "His car was headed downhill. She came up. When she got out, he decided she was what he was waiting for. So the question is, did he kill her because he thought she was Glenna, or did he kill her because he thought she was you?"

Chelsea shifted uncomfortably. "I dunno," she answered irritably. "I didn't know anybody was watching."

That's the trouble with people who are hiding things. They don't know when to come in out of the rain. Chelsea was starting to know fear, but she didn't want to say what her problem was because she was afraid the answer would be even worse. So she lied and dodged and trusted to luck that she wouldn't stab herself with the knives she juggled.

"It's your neck," I told her. "But if you want to play with snakes, you'd better hope they aren't diamond heads."

"I don't know what you're talking about. I don't know what my sister got herself into."

"All right," I said, "we'll play it your way. But if we do, you'd better not be caught by the police. Do you need to be told why?"

She said, "Who needs to be told not to get caught by the police?"

"Listen, then. I'm going to call the police. They're going to come here and look around and ask a lot of questions. I can answer their questions because I know how. You can't, because you don't know how. You believe me?"

She nodded, with large eyes that didn't say a thing. She said, "I believe you. I don't want to talk to the police."

"That's fine, then—*if* you mean it. Because if you mean it, I'm going to put you in my master bedroom and close the door. You are to stay there and not make a sound—and I mean, don't turn on the TV or the radio. Understand?"

She smiled. "I'm to be as quiet as a mouse."

"The police will talk to me. I'll tell them everything I can about your sister. I don't think it'll do much good, but they're going to want to know it all. It'll take a long time—if I know the police."

"I know, and I stay in your bedroom. What if the police do a search? Won't I be compromised?"

I laughed. "Where'd your generation learn that phrase? No, you're not compromised, you're put in jail." I leaned close to her. "Do you understand? In jail."

She looked hurt. "You don't have to threaten me. I don't want to go to jail."

"Fine, then stay there and don't make a sound. The cops won't look for you unless they hear you—know you're there. And once they do that...bye-bye, baby."

Chelsea shuddered. Partly it was what I said, partly it was the thought of her sister, dead at the bottom of the stairs. "Yes, all right," she told me, and I took her up to the bedroom, made her comfortable and then telephoned the police.

5

POLICE CAPTAIN PERRIOD MARSTAN rode out with the work crew. He's high in the department and doesn't have to dirty his hands with crime scenes, but he was on duty that night and didn't want to stare at the walls of his office. As he said to me when he arrived, "It's good to keep your hand in."

I was out there showing him what was left of Glenna Powers and he was scratching his cheek. The photographer was taking pictures and a detective named Lasky was making notes. It was Lasky's case, except where Marstan overrode him, and right then the police captain was in charge. He queried me and Lasky listened. I told them the girl's name, that the nearby convertible belonged to her. I told them what I'd heard and seen: the thudding sound, the girl falling down the stairs, and the Lincoln going off down the slope.

"Lincoln?" Marstan said. "You're sure it was a Lincoln? It was running without lights, you say."

"I caught it in the streetlight down below."

"But it was going fast." Marstan climbed enough of the steps to see over Glenna's car. He studied the blue white glow down there. "You were about here?"

"A couple of steps higher. It was a good view."

"And you're willing to swear it was a Lincoln?"

"I'm willing. Why? You know whose it is?"

"Hell, no," he said, "but I don't want to chase Lincolns and find out it was a Ford." He nodded at my digs. "How about going in where we can sit down?"

Lasky came with us and we settled in the living room, Perry with a beer I offered, Lasky with a glass of water. Perry looked around. "Nice place, Simon. Looks like private-eyeing pays off."

"It doesn't cost much to live alone."

Perry smiled expansively. "I'd like to try it sometime." He has a wife and three kids. "Now, about this Glenna Powers. She was a friend of yours?"

"She was a client."

Perry arched an eyebrow. "She was coming here on business?"

"That's right."

"How come not at your office?"

"It's after hours."

"You wanna tell me what kind of business?"

"No."

Perry knew the rules about confidentiality, but he wasn't happy. "There's been a murder here, Simon. I can't make you talk, of course, but if you've got evidence that can clear up this case, you know you're obligated to give it."

I said, "How can I tell you what she wanted to see me about if she was killed before she got here?"

He didn't have an answer and chewed on his lip. His eyes roamed, sizing up my living style, guessing how much I made and who might get shot wanting to tell me something. "Did she mention any enemies?" he said at last.

"No."

"She came to see you after hours. It was a life-and-death

matter. You agreed to see her. She had to have told you something."

He was being speculative and he was shrewd. He wanted what I knew, and he wanted it bad. But it wasn't anything that would help him, at least not yet, and I wasn't wasting anything on him. Glenna had been trying to save her sister, had been knocked off in the attempt. In fact, she'd probably been killed instead of Chelsea, so the least I could do was keep Chelsea on ice until I found out who was up to what. I said to Perry, stroking my chin and playing his own game, "Well, she did mention the name Ralph Scorwitch. That mean anything to you?"

Now it was Perry who was on the spot. He kept a poker face, but his eyes said he knew more than the name. "Ralph Scorwitch?" he said, arching an eyebrow.

"His name was in the paper today," I said. "He got murdered last night. I assume it's the same guy."

"Yeah," he said slowly. "There was a murder last night."

"What kind of an M.O. did the killer use? Maybe it's the same person?"

Perry didn't like it. He shook his head. "You're asking too many questions, Simon. I'm asking you questions about this death here, and you're trying to ask me about a killing last night."

"I'm wondering if they're related."

"That's for me to wonder about. That's what I get paid for, not you. I'm trying to find out about this death here. I wanna know what you know about this Glenna Powers. She got any relatives, family? You know where she lives?"

"Why the hell ask me? Look it up in the hall of records. You will anyway."

"That car you saw—that you think was a Lincoln—you saw it start up and go down the hill?"

I nodded and he said, "It didn't turn around or nothing?"

"No."

"So it didn't follow her up here. It was waiting for her to come. Someone had this place staked out. You're aware of that?"

"It's obvious."

"Who knew she was coming here—besides you?"

"I don't know. *I* didn't tell anybody, if that's what you're thinking." I gave him a twisted smile. "What do you think I do, set up my own clients?"

"Somebody knew she was coming here and was laying for her, but you say she didn't tell you what it was about?"

"That's right."

"She didn't say, 'Somebody wants to kill me. Will you protect me?' It wasn't protection she wanted?"

"No."

"She talked about Ralph Scorwitch? What'd she say?"

"Nothing. She said she wanted to see me about a man named Ralph Scorwitch and it was very important."

"You think she had information about his death she wanted to give you?"

"Certainly not. If she had information about his death, I'd expect her to take it to the police."

"She didn't think she was going to be killed, then?"

"That's pretty obvious."

"Maybe it's a case of mistaken identity."

"Come again?"

Perry was wearing a shrewd grin. "It's dark. All you've got is a light on your stoop. The guy in the Lincoln—or

whatever kind of car it is—is expecting someone to come
see you—a girl, let's say. And along comes a car and out
gets a girl. So he shoots her and takes off. But he shoots the
wrong girl. How about that for an angle?"

"That's very good," I said. "Except that that means I was
expecting another girl to come along. I entertain all my
women clients after hours at home."

He was watching me with hungry eyes, trying to read
behind the veil. "Maybe Glenna wasn't coming to consult
with you alone," he went on. "Maybe another girl was
coming, too."

"Except she changed her mind, or she saw all you cops
around and got scared away. Come on, Perry," I said irritably, "what're you trying to say?"

Perry smiled. He had me edgy and that's what he wanted.
"It's an interesting fact," he said, "that Glenna has a
younger sister by the name of Chelsea, and Chelsea looks a
lot like Glenna. Now if both sisters—"

"Oh," I interrupted, "so Glenna has a sister, does she?
She's younger and her name is Chelsea? How the hell did
you find all that out so fast? You've only been here twenty
minutes."

Perry had tripped himself. "Well," he mumbled, "it's just
information the department happened to have—"

"Happened to have? Then there *is* a connection between
her death and Ralph Scorwitch's? Spill it, Perry."

He was on the spot again and he didn't like it. He got up
and went out to check on the investigation.

That's the trouble with policemen friends. There are
things they've gotta hide from you, no matter how close
you are. And there are things you've gotta hide from them.

THEY TOOK GLENNA'S BODY AWAY at half-past eight, but the police weren't gone and the rubbernecking neighbors weren't back in their own condos and the coast wasn't clear until after ten. Meanwhile, Chelsea had been stashed in my bedroom and neither of us had had anything to eat but agony.

I went up there when the last of the police cars had pulled away and all that was left was Glenna's rattly convertible. It didn't figure in the case and the cops didn't want to get stuck with the cost of impounding it.

I opened the door and turned on the lights: all was silence. There wasn't any evidence that the room was occupied and right away I got nervous. Chelsea Powers was as predictable as earthquakes and I don't like it when I don't know which end is up. I called her name and looked around. I thought the bedspread might at least have been mussed, but it hadn't been touched. The calling and hunting got no response, but I knew she had to be in the room. Even the hand-crank window had to be opened from inside and the handle was in place.

I found her. It took a bit of hunting, but there she was under my bed, knees under her chin, hands gripping her shins, her eyes as bright as pennies.

I said, "All right, why didn't you tell me where you were?"

She just stared at me with her penny-bright eyes.

I stuck my head under the bed. "Chelsea, it's all right. They've gone."

I could have been talking to the moon.

I grasped her ankles, which were the nearest part of her, and dragged her out over the shag carpet. It's rough and scratchy and raised welts on her bare arms and on her thighs where her skirt rode up.

When I had her free, she stayed the same way. She was out in the light now, but her eyes were as blank as when she'd been spaced out the night before. Except this time she hadn't been into drugs. What was stabbing her psyche tonight was fear. She was all but catatonic.

I pulled her to her feet and sat her on the bed, but she didn't help. She looked at me as if I were some guru and she was just off the nut tree. I sat down beside her and held her hands. They felt like ice packs. I stroked her forehead and it gave me chilblains. "Chelsea," I said, "can you understand me?" If she didn't respond, it was into the hospital and let Perry Marstan hassle me if he wanted.

But an answer did come through. A sense of comprehension made the grade and she whispered, "Glenna's dead." She sounded like a ghost. Then she said it again and clutched my arm. "Simon, Glenna's dead."

She knew me, and she understood the situation. I could breathe once more.

"I know," I said, and held her close. "Hang on and don't go to pieces."

She clutched me and wept, great shudders going through her body. She cried with convulsive sobs, and there was nothing I could do except tighten my grip, kiss her hair and her cheeks and brush the tears from her face.

Eventually she pulled away and looked into my eyes. "Simon," she whispered, "she was my sister, and she's dead."

I nodded and stroked her back. "Did you love her?"

"I hated her. No," she sobbed. "I loved her. Of course I loved her."

I watched this strange creature whom I caressed. She didn't know who she was or what she wanted. Was she

flying high for a soaring experience, or was she only trying
to escape from a cage whose doors were always open?

It didn't matter. The pain she felt was real, whatever the
cause. She had cursed her sister and sworn to stay clear of
her, but now her sister was dead and she sang a different
song. Shock was a factor, and I had the feeling that the
difference would not long endure.

"You loved her," I conceded, stroking Chelsea's hair.
"She tried to be your mother, which was a pain in the neck
to you, but it was a pain in the neck to her, as well."

She slipped to the floor at my knee. "She was like my
mother," she said. "I thought it went with her nature. You
mean she didn't like it?"

"She hated it," I said. "She wished she could throw in the
towel—surrender. But she felt a responsibility to you. And
now you've got to feel one to her. She died trying to save
you, Chelsea. So you've got a big debt to pay."

She turned up a tearstained, puzzled face. "She died
trying to save me?"

I kissed her forehead and stroked her hair. "She was shot
by someone who thought she was you, by someone who
knew you'd be coming here. Who knew you were coming to
see me, Chelsea?"

She looked up with enormous dark eyes. "What?"

I let the idea simmer in her mind for a bit. "Think about
it," I said. "This place was staked out. Someone came here
to kill you tonight, just the way someone killed Ralph last
night. The difference is that tonight he missed you and got
your sister. Do you understand?"

The shudder that surged through her shook even the
soles of her feet. She understood.

6

I BUNKED HER in the guest room and she behaved herself. For once she had something on her mind besides sex and drugs.

I made her a big breakfast the next morning and told her she was going to be a houseguest for a while. She looked at me. "It's not what you think," I told her. "This is a precaution. Somebody's after your hide and you've got to keep it hidden."

"You mean I'm in jail?" Her face was marked with displeasure.

"It's better than a graveyard."

She shivered. I'd reminded her of her sister. "But I can't hide long," she said. "There's my sister's funeral."

"You're not going."

"I'm not...?"

"I'll tell you about it. You're not going there, you're not going anywhere. You're going to stay in a wall-to-wall carpeted jail."

Chelsea looked around in distaste. She hated being hemmed in. "What's there to do here?"

"Read books. Watch TV."

She glowered. "Very funny."

I know how to glower, too. I said, "Listen to me,

Baby June. Somebody out there—" I waved at the
world "—wants to kill you. I told you that last night. Now
I'll tell you why. He saw you when he killed Ralph Scorwitch and he thinks you saw him. He doesn't want you to
tell anybody what you saw. You get the idea?"

It glimmered. Chelsea wasn't the fastest brain in captiv-
ity, but comprehension was possible. "What if I said I saw
him?"

"It would help."

"Could I go home?"

"Don't play games with me, little sister. There are real
bullets out there. Glenna took three of them for you. Don't
make it in vain."

Chelsea was sufficiently shaken. She leaned toward me,
one elbow in a pool of slopped coffee. "Simon," she whispered, "I did see him." Her eyes were large and round, like
those of an awed and innocent child.

"What'd he look like?" I said. She knew more games than
Hoyle and I wasn't going to play them with her. Either she
backed up what she said or I'd give it the deep six.

"Dark hair," she answered, staring at me intently, willing
me to believe. "Swarthy face," she went on. "Very cold
eyes." She shivered. "That's why I didn't tell you before. He
scared me."

The description fitted the man in the Lincoln, but it
matched an army of people who never drove a Lincoln.
"What else?" I said.

"What else is there?"

That's what you get from the average citizen—an effect,
an aura, a sense—nothing you can hang a description on at
all. I didn't blame Chelsea. Considering the state her mind
was in, that was a first-class report.

I left her with the fear of God in her heart and checked in at the office. Eileen gave me eyes that seemed to smell a rat, but I gave her a face as innocent as Cain's. I don't know where she gets her ideas. I handed her the Lincoln's license number and said I wanted a make on the owner. She said, "How's the dark-haired stripper who was in here yesterday morning? The one whose buttons were all missing?"

"They weren't missing. She just likes to undo them."

"Same difference."

"Says you."

That held her, but only until she came back. "Hey," she said, wide-eyed. "You didn't tell me—the woman who was killed on your steps! Was that the one?"

"It was her sister."

Eileen swallowed. "Listen, kimo sabe, are you in trouble?"

Worry showed in her eyes. The trouble is, she dresses to show off her cleavage and you have to exercise effort to notice such things as her eyes—which are a beautiful green, I might add.

I shook my head. "Not yet. But I need to know a few things—like who owns that Lincoln."

She compressed her lips. "I don't think you're going to like it." She put the piece of paper with the owner's name in front of me and waited.

The Lincoln, according to her information—direct from the Motor Vehicle Department—belonged to H. Marshall Schyler III, and you have to live in my town to know what that means. H. Marshall Schyler III is grandson of the guy who made this town. I don't mean he built it; he developed it. He brought in the money and the influence and the other rich scions who brought in the artisans and built the factories and developed the culture and this and that and all the rest. The first H. Marshall Schyler even was mayor of the town, and he might have made governor except there were whispered scandals and evidences of indecencies here and there that caused a nomination withdrawal. Nothing was ever proved, mind you, but there was enough smoke to suggest a fire and the Schylers thought it wiser to smother their own blazes than to hand them over to the volunteer fire department.

So much for the first H. Marshall Schyler. Number II was much like the old man, a devoted follower of developing the town's assets, which in general coincided with the family assets. H. Marshall Schyler I made it big. H. Marshall Schyler II made it bigger. About H. Marshall Schyler III, not much was known. He lived on one of the great estates in town, he had inherited all the assets of his forebears and could wield great influence. Thus far, however, he had chosen to eschew the public eye, live within his own realm, spend his money without fanfare and keep a low profile. His name came up now and then in connection with certain causes or philanthropies, but for the most part he was unknown and unsung, and he was the last one in the world I would have expected the Lincoln to belong to.

I studied the paper for so long Eileen got tired of shifting her feet. "How bad is it?"

I looked up at her, past the cleavage to the green eyes. "You're sure the information is accurate?"

"It's courtesy of the latest M.V.D. computer printout. That's as far as I swear."

I patted her hip and a bit more, and she let my hand stray.

She's encouraging when you don't pet her enough, skittish if you pet her too much. I prefer to be encouraged so I underplay, but it's hard to know. We walk a narrow tightrope, she and I, and I'm not sure what her game is, nor is she sure of mine.

She said, "Is he involved in this?"

I got up and stuck the paper in my pocket. "I don't know," I told her, "but his car is."

"That doesn't make sense."

I put a finger on her nose. "When did the detective business ever make sense?"

THE H. MARSHALL SCHYLER ESTATE was at the crest of a hill three miles out of town and included a few of the surrounding hills, as well. Schylers I and II were money grubbers and into everything. They were the ones who had built and developed the estate, and at one time there'd been great write-ups about the lavish parties and high jinks that went on out there. That had all stopped when Marshall Schyler III inherited the keys to the kingdom. You almost forgot Schyler Manor existed.

I drove the heap up there in the early afternoon. I could have called for an appointment—Eileen thought that was the route to go—but there are times when I only listen to my own instincts, and they told me to use the unnatural approach. A car H. Marshall Schyler III owned was involved in a murder, at least in my book, and that meant forget the frontal approach. Move on the oblique.

There were gates and walls at the entrance to the estate that hadn't been there in the days of the earlier Schylers. In olden times there were drawbridges and moats. Today the defenses are more modern, but they say the same thing: only those who are welcome are let in.

And you don't get to be welcome by driving up and knocking on the front door.

Nevertheless I was there, the nose of my car prowling against the straight steel shafts of a chained and mighty gate. An eighteen-wheeler would buckle against those bars, so all I could do was halt and shut off my engine when the ugly man from the gatehouse came stalking forward, showing off his side arms.

His uniform was knife-edge black and gold, missing only the swastikas, and he looked as if starving children made him hungry. He came through a door in the gate, poked his head through my window and said, "Whaddaya want?" looking at my forehead as if that's where the bullet would go.

I gave him my card. "I was hoping to see Mr. Schyler about a car he owns."

Herr Storm Trooper read the card silently, except that his lips moved. He looked at me again. "You got an appointment?"

"No, but if you'll tell Mr. Schyler it has to do with one of his cars—a black Lincoln—he might give me one."

He returned to his cubbyhole, rereading the card suspiciously, and picked up the phone. In five minutes he was back. He didn't like it, but he opened the gate. "Stay on the main road," he said. "Otherwise you'll be in trouble."

I nodded and drove on through, but the idea that the murder car belonged to H. Marshall Schyler III didn't sound so farfetched anymore. Rich men need protection, but he wasn't Fort Knox. Something was out of whack.

The road was a two-laned paved highway that wandered through woods, bridged a lake, edged manicured lawns and finally deposited me in front of a slate terrace that fronted on a stone-faced domicile the size of Buckingham Palace.

Nobody was in sight, but by the time I had crossed the terrace and reached for the doorbell, the massive oak and iron door was pulled inward and an elderly gentleman in green and white livery let me in. The foyer was also slate, with a vaulted roof reminiscent of Chartres. There were stained-glass windows on both sides, but they were secular in theme, not religious. Depicted were lush nudes with long, tumbled hair, except that the hair didn't quite cover the right places. You got the best view where the low November sun cast the image on the opposite wall.

The butler noticed my glance and gave me a sad smile. "I will show you to the study," he said. "The master will join you there."

I took a final look at the reflection of the unclad, buxom belle and fell in behind him. "Who washes the windows?" I asked.

"I don't think you should joke, sir," my leader said. "Levity is not a characteristic of this house."

He didn't have to tell me. I expected Muzak funeral music to be piped into the rooms.

We walked through labyrinthian hallways for about a mile and a half and then the white-haired butler turned a wrought-iron handle and pushed open another oak door that revealed a dimly lighted room with a view of an enclosed courtyard through leaded windows. The room was small compared to what else I'd seen, but it would still hold a freight car comfortably. There were paneled walls, soft leather furniture, massive tables with bookstands on them and a marble fireplace above which hung a lighted oil painting of a Rubenesque woman removing her sandal. It was all she wore.

The old man left me there, closing the door behind. A few minutes of heel cooling followed and I spent the time evaluating the rest of the room. "Study" was what the butler had called it, but "library" might have been a better name. Interspersed among the panels were bookcases chock-full of tomes, most of them in tooled leather, some with cardboard bindings, with here and there a scattering of paperbacks. The books weren't just for looks; they could be and had been read. The subject matter was limited, but the treatment was broad. The books covered every imaginable aspect of one particular field—sex. There were porno books. There were nude art books, there were nude art porno books. There were treatises on sex, analyses of sex, analyses of the psychiatry of sex, of the physiology of sex, of the joys of sex, the problems of sex, the anatomy of sex. The old books had H. Marshall Schyler printed on the flyleaves, the newer ones were stamped H. Marshall Schyler II. The newest ones did not bear the name H. Marshall Schyler III, however. Their flyleaves were, conveniently or inconveniently, blank.

I was in the middle of my rummaging when the door opened and, to the accompaniment of a quiet whirring noise, a man came in. He was dark haired, somewhere in his early forties, obscenely handsome and exquisitely dressed, and he was sitting in an electrically powered wheelchair.

As the chair came in, he mashed a holdered cigarette in the receptacle fastened to the chair's arm. He exhaled a last breath of smoke, beamed at me as if he'd invited me from across the seas, and held out his hand. "My dear fellow," he said, "this is a pleasant occasion. Simon Kaye, is it? I know the name. And I'm Marshall Schyler, the fortunate object of your visit." He clasped my hand warmly. "And how shall we celebrate our meeting? Let me give you some refreshment so that we'll be comfortable when we get down to business."

The chair, which he steered with a handle, took him to a cabinet near the fireplace, which when he opened it revealed all the appurtenances of a drinker's dream bar, even to a tiny ice maker, a sink and a water faucet. "Allow me, sir," he said as graciously as any king. "What is your pleasure?"

It was hard to refuse when faced with both his array and his urgent insistence, but I tried. "It's a little early in the day, don't you think?"

"What has time to do with pleasure?" he asked. "You sound like Cotton Mather."

"You mean you drink at—" I looked at my watch "—three o'clock in the afternoon?"

"Or four, or five, or nine in the morning. What on earth does it matter? If drink gives me pleasure, why should I not have the pleasure? Am I to say, 'I must wait fifteen more minutes till the sun is over the yardarm,' or some such silliness as that?"

I said that while it did sound silly, particularly the way he said it, a certain amount of discipline in one's life was beneficial.

"Beneficial to whom, for what? Do you think it gets you into heaven faster? Is that why you do it? Or do you feel that the pleasure of the event is heightened if you have to wait for it? Or maybe you find pleasure in self-denial. There are those who do, but I must confess I am one of those who get much greater pleasure from doing than from not doing."

While he was going on he was juggling decanters and glasses, and when he had finished he turned and handed me one of two glasses, keeping the other for himself. "Now, then, try that," he said, "and tell me whether it's sinful for us to enjoy such a concoction merely because the clock strikes three instead of six."

I don't know what he'd put into our glasses, but it did taste ambrosial. But what else could I expect? Most of the names of his bottles I'd never heard of, and those that I had were beyond the reach of my purse.

"Well, now," H. Marshall Schyler said, motoring to the windows and a comfortable easy chair, "do sit down, Mr. Kaye, where we can enjoy the view while we talk. The sun is already half up the walls of this courtyard and it won't last much longer."

I sat down in the chair and remarked that the hospitality inside the home was quite different from that outside the home.

"I don't quite understand."

I told him about the gatekeeper's S.S. credentials.

Schyler dismissed him with a wave of the hand. "When one is rich, one is endangered. The best way to avoid threats is to be threatening."

"You're saying it's a pose?"

He smiled. "Remember Shangri-la, Mr. Kaye? A lovely oasis of peace and happiness, remaining so only because the surrounding mountains and harsh climate made it impossible for those on the outside to get in. Eden can exist only as long as the forces of evil are kept out. Adam and Eve fell from grace because the forces of evil had infiltrated that garden in the form of a snake." Schyler III gestured at the window and the dimming courtyard beyond. "I intend for no evil to creep in here." He smiled. "Do you blame me?"

I conceded it hard to believe that anyone who had it made would run the risk of losing it all. "Unfortunately," I said, "this is what a lot of people do—not just Adam."

Schyler arched an eyebrow. "Not just Adam? Are you suggesting he managed his own downfall? Do you believe he was not seduced?"

"He blames Eve, and Eve blames the serpent, but all that is buck-passing. If Adam had been alone in that garden and God had told him not to eat the apple, he'd have done it anyway. Tell us not to do something and we do it. It's the way we're made. I fight with a priest friend of mine about this almost every time we see each other."

"Do you believe, then, that any sensible man would run a risk when he doesn't have to?"

I nodded and said, "I've seen people who've won a thousand dollars on the turn of a card risk it all on the turn of the next card. And there's nothing extraordinary about it. People do it all the time."

Schyler smiled. "I suppose that's true," he said. "Perhaps it's the position I'm in," he added, indicating his wheelchair, "but I find myself the kind of person who doesn't like risks. Give me the sure thing every time."

"You seem to have made it pay off."

He raised his glass and took a sip. "You have a question about automobiles?" he said. "My gatekeeper was a little vague. Perhaps you would explain?"

"I'm interested in a small, black Lincoln." I gave him the license number. "According to the Motor Vehicle Department, it belongs to you."

He smiled. "I wouldn't be able to verify that for you," he said. "I have no idea of the license numbers on my cars."

"But you do have a small black Lincoln?"

"I used to," Schyler answered, "It was a runabout-type car. But I sold it several months ago."

"Not according to the M.V.D."

He shrugged. "Perhaps they made a mistake. Did you check for recent sales? It might not have been recorded."

I said I hadn't and he nodded as if that explained it all. He pressed a button on the side of his chair. "But since you're here, allow me to show you around. I think you'll find we live a very up-to-date and enjoyable life at Schyler Manor. We are rather exclusive, I'll admit, but it's like Shangri-la, as I said. Only those who can cut their way through the wall of thorns are privileged to enjoy its pleasures."

I said, "I thought the wall of thorns protected Sleeping Beauty, not Shangri-la."

"It's one and the same. What's the difference between kissing Sleeping Beauty and living in Shangri-la?"

The door to the study opened and there appeared in the entrance as lovely a woman as one could wish to see either in Shangri-la or behind a wall of thorns. She was dark haired, clad in flowing gowns, and entered with a stately grace that spoke of experience. She was no longer a child,

but she had acquired maturity early for she appeared still a
year or two short of thirty.

She smiled at me as she entered, but her attention was on
Marshall Schyler, for she went to him and kissed his brow.

"My dear," he said, "I want you to meet Mr. Simon Kaye.
Mr. Kaye is a detective and he's curious about a car I used
to have. Do you remember the black Lincoln?"

The lovely lady regarded me somberly and nodded.

"I sold it several months ago, if you'll recall," he went on,
holding and patting her hand.

She nodded again. "Yes, I know."

"Who bought it?"

"I have no idea."

"Oh, well, it's of small import." He patted her hand again.
"Mr. Kaye is our guest, Mona, my dear, and I have offered to
show him around. I wonder if you will do the honors for
me?" He smiled at me. "My wife," he explained, "has legs as
I have not and she serves as my emissary. I hope you will
forgive me if I put you in her care? She will give you a
properly conducted tour."

Mona Schyler gave me an inviting smile. "It would be a
great pleasure, Mr. Kaye."

7

WE WALKED DOWN HALLS and looked into rooms together—
the library, the music room, the art gallery—but all that
registered was the young woman beside me, the voluptu-
ous scent of her perfume, the way her body swayed
beneath the folds of her gown, her deliberate nearness, the
caress of her hand on my sleeve as she guided me or spoke
to me or just plain wanted me to know she was there. She
had an aura, a presence, and everything else became background. And she knew it. There was that slight pleased
smile, a secret pleasure behind the mask of dutiful wife,
and when you were with her you knew that neither of you
gave a damn about the library or the music room or the art
gallery or the fact that the mansion was constructed in
1904 at a cost of one and a half million dollars, or that it
took a staff of twenty to man it properly, and help was
devilishly hard to get these days. All you did was watch her
out of the corner of your eye, note the slenderness of her
hands and wrists and wish that the flowing robes she wore
revealed her more explicitly. And you found yourself wondering about the man in the wheelchair and what, if anything, he could do for her as a husband; and if it was
nothing, and she had married him only for position and

convenience, what she did about such needs; and whatever it was, did he know and did he care?

Of course, wondering gets you nowhere, so I interspersed talk about the family paintings and how hard help was to get with more intimate queries such as how long had she been married to H. Marshall Schyler, and how had they met?

Her answers were that she and Marshall had been married for two years; they had met at one of his dos. Marshall was always throwing dos—great galas for hordes of people, most of whom were strangers to him but belonged to the fringes of the coteries of which he was the central figure. Marshall, she told me, had a million friends and they came from all walks of life. Did I know he'd been involved in prison reform? He was into drug rehabilitation, ecology, the plight of the blacks in America, the problem of health care for the aged. You name it and he was into it—if it had a humanitarian aspect. There were some things he was against—totalitarianism, communism, fascism, drug addiction, alcoholism, prostitution, anything that exploited the human condition. It seemed that H. Marshall Schyler had all the right motives and all the proper responses. You kind of wondered why he wasn't down in Washington giving the president the benefit of his experience.

That told me about Marshall, but it didn't tell me about Mona and Marshall. I asked a couple of other leading questions but got the same recital—about him, not about her, or them—all the while being introduced to this and that new room of the house, each one empty.

"Marshall sounds like an A-1 guy," I finally sighed. "It must be great being around a man of such character."

"It does have its moments," she said.

That was a cryptic remark. What was also cryptic was her behavior. Mrs. Mona Schyler was as earthy as they come. It was in her touch, her scent, her swaying movement, her nearness, her desire to touch you. Did it mean she got nothing from Marshall, or did it mean she didn't get enough?

"So it has its moments?" I said, trying a last time. "Tell me some of them."

She gave me a glint from the corner of her eye. "Ah, Mr. Kaye, I can read your mind."

"I've got no depths to me at all," I said, "and the name is Simon."

"Simon?" She tried it out a couple of times. "You're a well-formed man, Simon."

"And how is Marshall formed?"

She laughed lightly and squeezed my arm. "Ah, Simon, you are entertaining."

"And, Marshall is—what?"

She smiled at me enigmatically. "If he is pleased with me, then I am pleased."

I gave up then. "What else is there to see around here besides empty rooms? Do you and Marshall live alone?"

Her laughter tinkled. "Oh, heavens no. Do you think Marshall did not live before me? He has daughters, they have friends. There is a full household of relatives and guests. They just don't come near Marshall. They have their own pleasures in their own places."

"This sounds like an interesting house. I was tempted to say 'menagerie.'"

"Menagerie is the word," she answered. "I don't mean his

daughters, of course, but when one holds a year-round open house, one does create something of a zoo."

"Who comes here, just freeloaders?"

"There are those, of course. There are always those. Money attracts them. But Marshall has more than money, and he collects other things, as well. You are a part of his collection."

I looked at her. "Come again?"

"You." She stopped and pointed to me. "You are here, no? I am introducing you to Schyler Manor, no? Why do you think I am doing this? Why do you think Marshall summoned me to give you the guided tour?"

This was not a rhetorical question. She expected an answer. "I have no idea," I said.

"Because," she explained, "he wants you to be a part of this party. You've been invited to become one, of the privileged persons he wants to keep on hand."

"And suppose I don't want to be kept?"

Mona shrugged. "It's no matter. You don't have to accept his invitation. All he's doing is extending it—and I should tell you that very few people receive such an invitation. It means you've made a particularly favorable impression on him."

"Why? What did I do?"

She smiled. "I have no idea. You would have to ask him. All I know is that he would like me to introduce you to our ways and tell you that we would be delighted to have you share them with us whenever and however you want."

What can you do with an invitation like that? I said, "Lead on, Guinevere."

How much actual living Marshall Schyler managed to

encompass, I didn't know, but the guests did damned well.
We took an elevator to a lower level, and things got lively.
There were not only rooms down there, there were people;
and the people, like the rooms, came in all shapes, kinds
and sizes. Sitting about a poker table in a smoke-filled
game room were slit-eyed brooding types who looked as if
they would cut a throat quicker than they'd shake a hand.
In another room some healthy-looking sporting types in
slacks and plaid shirts played pool with some healthy-
looking girl types in halter getups that showed a healthy
amount of skin.

The indoor swimming pool attracted the most people.
There was a bar on one side along with a table loaded with
a constantly replenished supply of tasty tidbits. There were
lounge chairs, racks of towels, an arched glass ceiling and
an Olympic-sized pool, in and around which frolicked a
good dozen boys and girls ranging from age twenty-five
down to the age of consent. The boys wore bathing trunks
of various styles and colors, the girls wore bikini bottoms
without tops, and a couple of the more broad-minded of
them had forsaken the bottoms, as well. There was a great
deal of splashing, laughing, pinching, pushing, tickling,
ducking and the other sorts of things that go on among
young people when their parents aren't around.

Mona, my tour guide, merely said that this was one of the
most popular spots in Schyler Manor, that it didn't usually
quiet down until three in the morning, and that the main
ailment of the young people was puckered skin.

The makeup of the group was mostly white, but there
were blacks and Hispanics in there, as well. I didn't see any
American Indians or Asiatics.

There was a sauna beyond the bar and Mona pulled open the thick wooden door to show me the inside. Half a dozen young people of both sexes were there, all of them nude, all of them fondling and petting each other while they cooked. Nor were they disturbed at the interruption. They said, "Hi," to Mona, gave me a blank stare and went on with what they were doing.

When we stepped back outside, a girl climbed from the pool and came over. She pushed her wet blond hair back over her ears and hitched up the tiny bit of green bikini bottom that barely covered the critical part of her anatomy. Her dripping breasts were an even tan all over, her nipples dark and puckered. Her eyes were a green that matched her bikini, and she had strong white teeth that showed a generous smile. She was a dish and she wanted me to know it, which was the reason for the hair pushing and the unnecessary hitching of the front of her bikini bottoms. She wanted to make sure I didn't miss any of her charms.

"Mona, darling," she said. "Who is this divine hulk?" Her eyes ate me up.

Mona laughed. "It's your father's latest protégé, Sally, dear. His name is Simon Kaye, and you'll have to keep your hands off. I'm only giving him the tour."

"How long do I have to keep my hands off?" she sighed, sliding her palms up and down her thighs. "Would you like to go for a swim, Mr. Kaye? The water's fine."

I said, "It sounds delightful, Miss Schyler. Next time I'll bring my suit."

"No need. It's more fun without."

Another girl came over, a statuesque brunette, taller than Sally, not as amply endowed, but a girl who moved with a sinewy grace that carried its own invitation. She, like Sally, wore a bikini bottom, but it was black and a little less immodest. She might not have any more reservations than Sally at showing her breasts, but you'd have to wait a little longer to get at the rest of her.

She was Schyler's other daughter, by a still earlier wife, and her name was Carla. She studied me soberly during introductions and her eyes weren't the undressing kind like Sally's. She was more interested in the real me—my occupation and how I came to know her father.

I told her I was a detective making inquiries and that I didn't know her father. "He's a very kind man," I said. "I'm only here because he takes pity on homeless waifs."

"You ought to see the kind of pity I take on homeless waifs," Sally said.

Mona laughed. "Down, Fido. You have to let him get used to you first."

Sally said to me, "You will come again? You must."

"I'm sure I will," I said as Mona pulled me away. When we went out the door, Carla was back by the pool in the company of some man, but Sally was where we'd left her, hand on hip, looking after us broodingly.

"So those are Marshall's daughters?"

"The two and only. Attractive, aren't they?"

"All the women in this house are attractive, wives as well as offspring."

"We share a lot in common, the three of us. Sally is the more predatory, however. She goes after what she wants."

"I noticed she files her teeth."

"She may give you trouble."

"I'll go into training."

The tour ended back in Marshall's study. He was still there, poring over a book, and he looked up brightly. "Well, sir," he said with a fond glance at his young and comely wife, "while I can't vouch for the interest my estate may hold for you, I'm sure that, with my wife as guide, you did not find it dull."

I said, "'Dull' is, I think, the last word I would use to describe anything with which you are connected."

He was delighted. "Well put. You know my weakness. I am a total slave to flattery. Stroking my ego is like Aladdin stroking the lamp. Whatever you wish for is yours." He put the book aside and swung his wheelchair around. "But now," he said, "how shall we entertain you till dinner? You will stay, of course? And in the meantime, what is your pleasure? If you would care to ride horseback .... "

If you didn't get up and go, the guy would smother you. It was like marshmallow whip with nuts and chocolate sauce and a cherry on top. Let yourself go and you could sink into a tasty, delightful hedonistic limbo, come up for air twenty years later and never know the time had passed. It was like a chocolate-coated Las Vegas, the place of no clocks and no closing times. The difference here was that besides the gambling there were other lures—booze, sex, comfort, excitement, all right on the premises, all safe inside the unbreakable gates. I noticed, now that I thought about it, that I hadn't seen a clock in Schyler Manor, either. Time mattered only to people who had to punch clocks.

I stood up, because it was easier to say no that way. "I really appreciate this, Mr. Schyler," I said.

"Please. My name is Marshall, and yours is Simon. We do not stand on ceremony here."

"Fine, and thank you, Marshall." I then explained that I had to leave because I was, after all, a working stiff and there were things I had to do, people I was responsible for, and all that. I would, however, be most delighted to take advantage of his hospitality another time.

Marshall assured me that it would come to pass, and Mona saw me to the front door.

8

IT TOOK A LITTLE WHILE to come down out of the clouds. You get caught up in that kind of nirvana and you wish the rest of the world would go away. I got into my car and sat in front of the steering wheel and thought about the swimming pool and all those luscious nude and seminude female bodies, and the orgasmic uses to which the sauna was being put. It was easy to wish I were one of those young studs populating Schyler Manor with no more problems than deciding which female to bang next or how many more times that day he could perform.

It was lotus land, but that was what was wrong with it. It was too easy to surrender and let the rest of the world go by. I had a feeling it wasn't really for me. I even had a feeling that I'd get bored in time. It would be fun to conduct the experiment, but the trouble was, if I found I'd made a mistake it would be too late to correct it.

I had to pull myself together.

Now, then, I decided, as I started the engine and shifted gears, I'd been shown all the parts of Schyler Manor I was meant to see. I was like an American official being shown what life is like in Communist Wonderland. He sees only the dimples and the smiles. He doesn't see the pimples and tears. Marshall Schyler had accepted an unknown prying detective into his inner sanctum, had dismissed the detective's question with the most casual of answers, then sought to seduce the detective by throwing him in the company of a most alluring and seductive wife who showed him an alluring and seductive life-style. Now, an hour and a half after our meeting, Marshall and I were on a first-name basis and I'd been handed a passport to the kingdom. That made even less sense than the guard letting me through the gate in the first place.

I didn't go back out the driveway right away. I took the other route, behind the mansion to where the garages were. They were discreetly hidden so as not to spoil the view, but they weren't any secret. There were nine stalls in all, including a couple of lifts, and they were shaped in a curve around an apron that could have handled a 747. A row of gas pumps extended the arc, there was a drainage grate in the center of the apron to catch the wash water, and there were four vehicles on hand, three in the stalls, one outside. The one outside was an executive Caddy and it was being soaped and hosed by a short, squat man who had a face that came from a zoo.

As for the cars in the stalls, none looked familiar, but when I did a swing around on the apron I saw, tucked away in a middle stall a Chrysler wagon that had the black Lincoln's license plates on it. The Lincoln was gone, but the plates were there.

I didn't make the circuit uninterrupted. The squat creature pampering the Cadillac yelled "Halt!" and stalked over. I halted and let down a window to see what I could find out.

"Who the hell are you?" he said, eyeing me like a repossession man.

"Interesting array of cars you've got here," I said. "What happened to the Lincoln?"

He wasn't buying it. "I said, who the hell are you? Lemme see your license."

I said, "Say, does Marshall know how you treat his guests?"

He pulled open my door. "Get outta the car."

There comes a point. I could put on as steel-eyed a look as he, and I did. "If I get out," I said, "you're not going to like it."

It was steel against steel, but he wasn't just looking, he was calculating—my weight, my heft, my condition, the size of my muscles. If he'd had a spanner wrench in his hand it might have been different, but he wasn't even holding his hose. He slammed the door on me and pointed. "Get the hell outta here," he ordered, "and if you ever come back, you'd better bring a coffin."

"Up yours," I told him cheerfully and drove out. In the mirror I could see him standing, hands on hips, glowering after me. But it wasn't all glower. He looked a mite shaken, as well.

The last I saw of him, he was heading to a wall phone inside one of the bays.

I went back to the office analyzing what I'd found. I wasn't wrong about the license plates. Two days ago they'd been on a black Lincoln a block from the Powers's house. This afternoon they were adorning a Chrysler station wagon. Marshall claimed he'd sold the Lincoln some months ago, but this morning the M.V.D. had it listed in his name. So you pays your money and you takes your choice.

How much did Marshall Schyler know about Chelsea and Glenna? What did he know about Ralph Scorwitch's murder? Was Ralph a supplier? Was there bad blood? No use pretending Marshall Schyler III was some kind of innocent victim, not after the welcome mat he threw me. Even philanthropists ask for credentials before they distribute their largess. Marshall hadn't asked for a thing.

I walked into my reception room frowning and Eileen made a face. "I don't know why handsome lady killers have to look glum," she said. "You ought to be jumping for joy — off the roof!"

I made a face that equaled hers. "What particular lady am I killing this afternoon?"

Eileen pulled over her pad, but she didn't have to read the name: she had it memorized. "A Chelsea Powers — I'm sure you remember the braless wonder of yesterday morning? She telephoned at two forty-five, at three twenty-three, at three forty-two, four-oh-nine and four twenty-five." Eileen looked at her watch. 'It is now four forty-three and a half. She is probably dialing again this moment." She put her hand on the phone dramatically and prepared to lift the receiver.

"And what was her message?"

"She didn't leave any. Her words are for your ears alone."

"Three twenty-three, three forty-two, four-oh-nine! Your accuracy in recording phone messages puts you, as secretaries go, in a class by yourself."

"I don't want you to miss any nuances, you being a detective and all."

"Thanks, and speaking of nuances, did you deduce any from all these calls?"

"Yes," she said. "They had the urgency of a woman who has just discovered she is with child."

I went into the office on that one. Eileen is not someone to match words with.

I dialed home, let it ring twice, hung up and dialed again. Chelsea answered with a singsong, "Detective Kaye's answering service."

I said, "Good. Did you think that up all yourself?"

"You said I couldn't be too careful. Where the hell have you been?"

"Detecting. Why? What's the problem?"

"The problem is staring at your goddamned four walls. I've got to split or go crazy. My sister's in the morgue, a killer is on the loose, you're out detecting, and I'm left with nothing to do but sweat. You didn't even leave me a joint. What're you trying to do, drive me nuts?"

I said, "Hold the fort, sweetheart, I'll be home in a jiffy."

"I'll expect you by half-past five. Otherwise look for me at the funeral parlor. I'll be visiting Glenna."

The trouble was, she could. The ramshackle convertible was still parked outside my door. I don't like ultimatums, but what're you going to do? "I'll be there," I yelped.

OF COURSE there had to be the usual last-minute items that always come in when you're in a hurry: the call from the client who wants a detailed progress report while the minutes tick away, the letters you have to read and sign because they must go out that night, the fact that the attendant has to move four cars to get yours out of the lot.

I did the best I could, but it was still quarter of six and pitch-dark when I pulled into my angled slot. From the bottom of the hill I could see there were no lights in my place, but the convertible was unmoved and that made me feel better. All the same, I took the steps two at a time and had my key at the ready when I reached the top.

I opened the door and the place was inky and silent. Turning on the foyer light didn't help much. It threw a dull amber glow that was swallowed up by the rooms beyond. I kept wondering about the missing Lincoln and the swarthy guy who had been driving it.

Then there was movement in the distance and Chelsea Powers came into view. She had changed clothes and was now wearing one of my pajama tops, the sleeves reaching almost to the tips of her fingers, the bottom hem hanging just low enough so that you couldn't quite see anything, except sometimes you could. "It seems," she said, "all I ever do is wait for you to come home."

She looked so good I threw my briefcase onto a chair, picked her up in my arms and kissed her. And not because she looked so fetching in my pajamas, but out of relief that she was all right. That's not to say the pajamas weren't part of it. She was cute as hell and sexy as hell at the same time, and I don't know how long you think I can hold off from that sort of thing.

So I kissed her and she threw her arms around my neck to kiss me back and held on so that when I let her slip back down, my head had to come down, too. I started to pat her fanny, but the pajama top had ridden up so high her fanny was bare, so I let the patting go and undid her arms. "Now we have to talk," I told her.

"Why?"

I pulled the pajama top down into place all around. "Because you give me heart failure," I said, and went into the kitchen to make a drink. "I want to keep you safe.

You're in danger and you don't seem to grasp that. Would you like to booze it up with me for a bit?"

"I might as well do something for entertainment around here. You sure don't provide very much."

"I've got a lot of things on my mind."

"You've got too goddamn many things on your mind if you want my opinion."

I poured her some rye and soda, half and half, then decided to make it three-quarters rye. We went down into the living room and turned on lights. She sat primly on the couch, knees together, an elbow on each, holding her drink in both hands, taking tiny sips. I took the facing chair and took big sips and asked her if she'd ever heard of H. Marshall Schyler, and she hadn't. I asked if Ralph Scorwitch had mentioned him, and he hadn't, either. She didn't know who H. Marshall Schyler was. I told her he owned a Lincoln that was driven by a man who matched her description of Ralph Scorwitch's killer.

It didn't impress her. She yawned and sat back, tucking one foot under the other knee. That way the pajamas didn't have a chance. From the waist down she showed off everything.

I sighed, finished my drink, put down the glass and got up. I went over, took her glass from her hand and set it on the end table. Then I stood her up, unbuttoned the pajama top and threw it open, off her shoulders. Her breasts jutted out prettily and I fondled them. She said, "Why, Simon, I never thought you cared," and let the pajama top fall to the floor.·

We went up to the bedroom, she running ahead like a tot anxious for her Christmas stocking. Without going into details, I have to say she was some doll! She exploded five times in less than an hour and a half, and I mean she exploded. Half the time I hardly had to do more than touch her. She had the hottest pants of any girl in town.

I played it cool, myself, as cool as I could, that is, for she could do things to you you wouldn't believe. Anyway, I was conserving myself for the long haul. I didn't know how much she'd want or for how long. For a while there, she couldn't get enough.

Between times I brought her her drink and we'd both take a sip now and then. Finally, along about quarter of eight, either from rye or exhaustion, she went out like a light. She was zonked flat on her back, covered with a thin film of sweat, and if it weren't for her shallow breathing she could've been dead. I know all this makes me sound like sex king of the hill or the world's greatest lover, but I can't take the credit. She was primed and on a hair trigger.

I left her there in the semidark room, got back into some clothes, checked to make sure the place wasn't being staked out again, then scrambled myself some eggs in the kitchen. I hadn't exhausted myself the way she had and I was hungry.

I was in the middle of the eggs, a salad and a beer when the phone rang. I picked up the kitchen extension and it was Marshall Schyler III, no less.

"My dear boy," he said in contrite tones, "I owe you the profoundest apology. I only just this minute discovered it."

"Discovered what?"

"You asked me this afternoon about a Lincoln automobile you said was registered to me, and I told you I'd sold it some time ago. You recall?"

I said I did.

"I'm sorry to say I was wrong. It was not sold; I'd thought

it was. I'd ordered it put on the market and had assumed—
well, through a mix-up it hasn't been sold and it still
belongs to me. Unfortunately, I now find it's been stolen.
I've just reported this fact to the police and wanted to make
amends to you."

He apologized again for misleading me and accepted full
responsibility for the error. What was it I wanted to know
about the automobile?

"Do you know when it was stolen?"

"I have no idea. Neither do any of my garagemen,
because of the mix-up—between selling and stealing. It
wasn't until I checked on it after talking to you that we
discovered what had happened."

"That's a rather gross oversight, I might say."

"I know," he said humbly. "I must confess my garagemen
aren't the best. But that's my responsibility." He brightened. "But tell me, does this help you at all? Are you
working on a case?"

I said, not really, I was just checking something out.

He laughed. "You detectives are always so close-
mouthed. I hope whoever stole the Lincoln hasn't
been using it in a way that would get me in trouble?"

I said he couldn't prove it by me, and he sounded
relieved.

"That's good," he said. "And now my daughter would like
to speak to you."

The next voice I heard said, "Hi, this is Sally. We met this
afternoon, remember?"

Who could forget? I said, "Yes, I remember."

"I'm the blond one. My sister, Carla, has dark hair."

"I noticed that," I said, "among other things."

Laughter tinkled. She liked that. "We're having a great

party here tonight. We'd like you to come. Bring a pair of pajamas and a toothbrush."

"I'm tied up tonight," I said, "thanks all the same." I was looking at the steps to the master bedroom and thinking of Glenna in the funeral parlor. Somebody had to think of those two girls.

"Tomorrow night, then?"

"That must be some party!"

"Surely you can make it tomorrow night?"

If I said no, would the guy in the Lincoln be wondering why? If I stayed too close to home, would he suspect I was hiding Chelsea? That was the last thing I wanted.

"I'll try to," I said. "What time?"

9

WHEN I WAS THROUGH with the meal I put the dishes in the sink, turned out all the lights, made sure the Lincoln wasn't in sight, locked the door and drove the heap down to the funeral parlor where Glenna was on view. Her plain gray coffin was in a small side room in the back, out of the way of two big wakes in the front parlors. There was the open casket, a vase of flowers on a table beside it, and a dozen chairs. A thin signature book bearing half a dozen names was on a lectern in the hall beside the door. I added mine, using a pen on a chain, and went inside. A baby spotlight shone on Glenna's face and the rest of the room was so dim most people would have entered for their moment with Glenna and gone out again without noticing the two dark-suited figures sitting in the back row. I saw them because I learned long ago to look in the shadows first. One was Father Jack, the other, Captain Perry Marstan.

I let my eyes pass quickly over Glenna's form and concentrated on the flowers. That's because I don't care to look at the corpses of my friends. I don't pray, either, so I stood there and thought sad thoughts about the futility of her fate and I wished her better luck in her new adventure. Then I went to the rear and took a chair between Jack and Perry. "Where'd the flowers come from?"

Jack said he'd provided them.

"That's nice. I'm sure she appreciates it. How long've you been here?"

"About half an hour. I thought she might be lonely. But a few people have come in—neighbors."

"Nobody from the telephone company where she worked?"

"I understand they're coming to the service tomorrow."

"What's going to be done with her?"

Perry spoke up. "She's going to be cremated."

Jack said, "I'm opposed."

"Why? She wasn't a Catholic, was she?"

"No, but I'm opposed anyway."

"What's the difference? Ashes to ashes."

He wasn't going to get into a theological argument with me there and he just shook his head. I said to Perry, "Why are you here? Hoping the murderer will return to the scene of the crime?"

"Or maybe the sister."

"My guess is little sister has crossed about three state lines by now," I suggested.

"Why?"

"If little sister does a vanishing act and big sister gets murdered, it doesn't take much brains to guess little sister saw it coming. If that's why she vanished, I'd expect her to stay vanished."

"You never know," Perry said.

"Find out who owns the Lincoln?"

"Alleged Lincoln."

"That answers my question. Any connection between her murder and Scorwitch's?"

"We got nothing that points to it."

"Except that Glenna mentioned his name, and you know about her little sister named Chelsea. What do you want Chelsea for anyway?"

"Routine questioning."

"About Scorwitch? She *is* involved. There is a connection."

Perry made a face. "Don't go reading too much between the lines, Simon. It's a good way to fall on your face."

I didn't have a good comeback so I got up, said, "It's been nice," and walked out.

I pulled into my slot in front of the condo and had to pass Glenna's convertible to get to my steps. It made me think too much and I wished I'd left the outside light off. There was no black Lincoln lurking across the way, but I still felt naked and exposed going up the stairs.

I let myself into the foyer and didn't turn on the light. I stayed just inside the door, shutting it quietly, and listening. The windows there and in the kitchen are uncurtained because nobody can see in, so there was enough light for me to get around. I checked the kitchen and dining room, then went up the stairs to the master bedroom. Chelsea was where I'd left her, a pale, white form stretched out on top of the bed looking like a waxen image. I kneeled on the mattress to put a hand on her forehead. She didn't move, but she was still perspiring and her skin was warm. For a moment she'd looked like a corpse and I needed the assurance that she was alive and unharmed. All was well, the sanctum sanctorum was unbreached. Why, then, did I feel so uneasy?

I went back down the stairs, still without lights, and groped my way into the sunken living room. There the darkness was really thick, for that's where I kept the curtains drawn. The windows face the sloping woods beyond on the same level, which means that snoopers could see inside. It was quiet and empty down there, but I couldn't get away from the unease that filled the place.

I found the padded bench in front of the windows, kneeled on it and parted the curtains enough for a look.

Nothing showed except a flat velvet darkness. The stark November woods were cold and barren; not a hint of movement came through the window. I kept staring, trying to make out the form of the nearest maple, and then I saw it, dead ahead—the tiny pinprick of light that's made by the glowing end of a cigarette. It brightened, moved, disappeared and returned. Whoever was watching in the woods had taken a drag and was taking another.

I had company.

Okay, but that was for tomorrow's agenda. I wasn't going to do anything about it tonight in the dark. Never go into the other guy's parlor. Set him up for yours.

I went up to the bedroom, and the only difference was, when I took off my holster, I stuck the gun in the bed-table drawer. Then I got out of the rest of my clothes, picked up Chelsea and slid her under the covers with me. It was like going to bed with a rag doll.

THERE WERE FIFTY PEOPLE at Glenna's funeral service: her friends and neighbors, her co-workers at the telephone company, plus a few unaffiliates such as Perry Marstan, Jack McGuire and me. The only person who didn't show up was Chelsea. She was just coming to when I left the condo and that was the way I wanted her. I'd have chained her to the bed if she'd talked about going.

I went in company with Jack. He told me my presence

proved I wasn't the heartless wretch I claim to be. I told him I was only there in case Chelsea appeared, to protect her from Perry.

He said, "Where do you think Glenna is at this very instant? In that coffin?"

I said, "No, but she isn't in hell, either."

"I don't think anybody's in hell."

"Even Hitler?"

"Even Hitler."

"I'm going to talk to your bishop about you."

"Do you know, the only reason you don't belong to a church is because you're not a joiner."

"How now, Mr. Freud?"

The service was nondenominational. Nobody knew what faith, if any, Glenna professed. Jack said she wasn't a Catholic, and he'd know. They keep records. Nobody else knew anything.

When it was over I asked Perry, "Did Chelsea show up?" His glower said I ought to know better. Perry doesn't have a great sense of humor.

I checked in at the office next, looked over the report from a security firm that was doing a job for me, phoned the people Eileen had on her call slips, and dictated three letters. Then I went home and walked around the back of the condo where the woods are. With the leaves gone, you couldn't hide a toothless comb out there and whoever'd been staking out the house the night before either had gone or was spying from cover somewhere else. In either case, the woods were empty and I went up to where, as best I could judge, I'd seen the lighted cigarette.

It didn't take long to find the spot. Almost a dozen Viceroy stubs littered a five-foot radius near the base of one of the trees. I didn't know who was staking me out, but he sure as hell was no pro.

I walked on, looking for the disturbed leaves, footprints and broken twigs that would trace his path. The trail led me back over the rise and out the other end of the woods a hundred yards away where nature surrendered to the back side of a shopping center. There was blacktop all around, including the area behind the stores, so there was no way to discover where his car had been, what kind of tire marks it left, and so on. But it would be a place to drive through on my way home at night, just in case a black Lincoln with phony marker plates was sitting around empty.

I returned to the condo and let myself in. Chelsea was up at last, rummaging in the kitchen. She met me in the foyer, threw her arms around my neck and gave me a big kiss. She was wearing what she had on the last time I saw her, which was nothing at all. When she let me go, I said, "My God, don't you ever take a breather?"

"What?"

I indicated her very bare pelt. "Your indoor sports costume."

"Oh, for heaven's sake," she said, going back to the kitchen, "I'm not interested in sex. I want some food. I'm starved." She looked in the refrigerator. "There are," she told me as she poked around, "other things in life than sex."

"You're very young to make such a remarkable discovery, but if your interest is elsewhere, you could at least put on some clothes. Walking around like that is like waving a flag in front of a bull."

She took out the milk and a bowl of canned peaches. "I'm not waving flags. I just feel comfortable without clothes."

"Well, the men who get to admire you don't. You have to

understand your costume is geared for bedrooms, not kitchens."

She put her hand on her hips. "That's the thing I can't understand about you men. Let a girl show a patch of skin—any old patch of skin—and the guy is beating down the door to get at her. You can show me skin—you can show me everything you've got, for that matter—and if I'm not in the mood, I couldn't care less."

"That's the difference. Boys are boys and girls are girls and never the twain shall meet—well, let's say, never the twain shall understand each other."

"A couple of days ago I couldn't get you to touch me. Now I can't keep you off me unless I put on some clothes. I hope they bar you from nudist camps. You'd be a raging bull. God help the mothers and daughters. I'll bet you'd be like Mrs. O'Leary's bull that set the whole of Chicago on fire!"

"Mrs. O'Leary's bull?" I took her in my arms and kissed her. "You know," I said, "someday I'd love to read your high-school history notes. Now eat your peaches and drink your milk and keep up your strength."

"Oh, the hell with that," she said. "You've got me all hot again." She took me by the hand and pulled me upstairs.

10

IT'S ALL WELL AND GOOD to have your own little sex kitten ready and waiting in your own little condo, but it has its drawbacks, too. You feel obligated to show up at the condo on some kind of regular schedule—like for breakfast, lunch and dinner—and frankly, the condo was the place I changed clothes in, took a bath in and sometimes slept in. In short, I only went there when I couldn't find any other place to go. Granted that Chelsea made the place a little more attractive, gave it that lived-in look; still and all, I can't stand being tied down and there are, sometimes, other things I like to do with my evenings besides play house with some girl—including conversation and chess with Jack McGuire. Then, too, there's my work; that at which I make my living.

Also, someone was keeping watch on the condo, which meant I shouldn't change my habits. In short, I was starting to feel tied to the place and I didn't like it.

Eileen sensed my change of mood back at the office. She came in for something from the files and looked me over. "*Qué pasó?*" she queried. "Somebody dent your fender?"

"What?"

"You're frowning, you're looking out the window, you aren't concentrating."

"How do you know what I'm doing? You're supposed to be in the outer office."

"I have been for the past fifteen minutes, but I notice you're on the same page of that report as the last time I came in."

"The girl's a detective."

"I've been working for you long enough. I'm getting to know how it's done."

I told her she was right, I wasn't concentrating, I needed some fresh air. I went down to the heap, tooled it around a few blocks, then took a ride over to the shopping center behind the condo. It was only four o'clock and still light and I wasn't expecting much but, damn it, a small black Lincoln was parked in the loading area behind the stores. The plates were wrong, of course, but the car was right, and all you had to do was walk from it up over the rise and you'd be looking into my condo windows. That's about as bush league as smoking cigarettes on a stakeout in the dark.

I pulled in behind the Lincoln and checked it over. Nobody was in sight, or course. The driver was over the rise keeping watch on my place, littering the woods with more of his butts. He hadn't even locked the car. I wondered if he knew it had been reported stolen.

There was nothing in the front or back seats. The glove compartment yielded only a flashlight and a registration made out to H. Marshall Schyler III, listing the license number that was now on his Chrysler wagon.

There were a number of things I could do: call the police to pick it up, sit around and wait for the driver to come back, or I could jump in the lake. The hell with all that.

Some guy was butting into my life and I get impatient about such things. I took a stroll up into the woods to see if it was who I thought it was.

He heard me coming; I wasn't trying to pussyfoot. And he didn't try to hide. I don't know if he expected it to be me or not, but he was facing me, his back to the condo, his fingers adjusting his fly. It was the sallow-faced, ugly-eyed lad who went with the Lincoln—the one who fitted Chelsea's description of Ralph's killer.

Normally I'm calm, cool and collected, but he made me see red. I didn't even try to pretend. "What the hell are you doing here?" I said.

He let go of his fly and hitched his pants—more of his call-of-nature act—but he wasn't intimidated. "Who's asking?"

He was ready, but he wasn't ready enough. He wore a jacket and heavy sweater and I'd already sized up the bulges. I knew where his gun was and where his hands were, and I didn't give him a chance.

I lifted him by his lapels and rammed him against a tree, shoved my forearm against his throat and had his gun before he'd even got his hands out of his belt. The gun was a duplicate of the .38 with silencer I'd seen in Scorwitch's apartment, and it would make the kind of thumping sound I'd heard when Glenna got shot.

He couldn't breathe well, the way I'd pinned him, but he had a lot of scrap in him—like a cornered rat. He tried to give me the knee in the groin, but I gave him mine instead. He screamed and sank to the ground, writhing, twisting, moaning and clutching himself. It wasn't a fair fight—I was bigger, stronger and more experienced than he—but it wouldn't have been fair whatever his size. He was the kind who's only a he-man until you take his hardware away. Then he's naked and yellow.

I yanked him up and held him against the tree again, clutching him by the throat with one hand and frisking him with the other. He had a switchblade in a pocket and a shiv in a scabbard strapped to one leg. I pocketed them, threw him on the ground and let him writhe around while I went through his wallet. There was sixteen hundred in cash in it, and a driver's license made out to Jud Lorne at—surprise, surprise—Marshall Schyler's address. The rest of what he had was a bunch of keys, some change, a pen, a pencil, a pack of Viceroys and a blank note pad. What he didn't have was a license to carry a gun.

I clapped handcuffs on him—a souvenir from my cop days—and pulled him to his feet. He sagged and tried to stay down. He was still moaning, but it was different now. He wasn't as bad off as he was pretending. I yanked him up by the scruff of the neck, grabbed him by the seat of the pants and marched him down to my car.

I took him down to the police station and by that time he could walk. Brad Walker was on the desk and he said, "What the hell?"

"Here's something to dry-clean," I said. I put the .38 with silencer on the desk. "That came out of his holster, here." I opened Jud's jacket to show him. "This switchblade came out of that pants pocket, this shiv and scabbard and straps came off his right leg. Here's his wallet. No license for the gun. Here are his keys. This one fits the ignition of a black Lincoln reported stolen by Marshall Schyler. The license plates are different, but that's because he switched them with another of Schyler's cars. I won't swear to it, but I'll give you three to one that bullets from that .38 will match the slugs that were put into Glenna Powers."

Brad gave a low whistle, pulled over the blotter and started to write. To Lorne, he said, "You got anything to say?"

Lorne, said, "I want a lawyer."

Perry Marstan came out of his office, looked at Lorne, looked at me and said, "What the hell is this about?"

I told him that's what Brad had asked, then gave him the same blow-by-blow account. When I reported that I'd picked Lorne up in the woods spying on my condo, Perry said, "You've been a busy little boy."

Lorne spoke for the first time. "What's he talking about, my spying on him? I never saw him before."

I said to Perry, "You might ask him about that Lincoln he's got the keys to. It's listed on your blotter as stolen from Marshall Schyler. Schyler called it in last night."

Perry nodded. "Lincoln?" he said.

"A dead ringer for the car that left the scene after Glenna Powers was shot."

"And you think the bullets will match this gun?"

"I'm offering three to one if you want to bet."

Perry shook his head. "I don't bet in the other guy's casino." He picked the gun up, told Sergeant Walker to give him an ID tag for it and he'd check it out. "Of course," he said in parting, "you know what silencers do to bullets."

I said I knew.

Lorne wasn't talking without a lawyer and they put him in the holding tank. I had to give a full statement and wait for it to be typed for signing. That's the trouble with getting involved with the mechanics of police work. It takes time, a lot of time. Time and paperwork. The paper was theirs, but the time was my own and if it weren't for the fact that Jud Lorne was a threat to life and limb, I'd have been ready to chuck the whole thing.

It was after seven when I got out of there and I didn't have many kind words for police routine, let alone people like Jud Lorne. I checked the back of the shopping center on my way home to see that the Lincoln had been picked up, and it was half-past the hour by the time I put a key in my door lock. Lights were on all over the place, which made me glad Lorne was no longer staked out in the woods. He wouldn't have to wonder where Chelsea was. She was advertising it.

She had some clothes on for once—the dress she'd arrived in —and she got up from the kitchen table as soon as she heard me. "Well, where the hell have you been?" she said, sounding just like a wife. "Do you know what time it is?"

"I'm often late," I said. "Sometimes I don't get home at all."

She didn't look kissable, what with her frown, and I glanced around the kitchen. There was a cereal bowl, milk and some gloppy eggs on a plate. "I'm glad you got something to eat."

"What the hell else is there to do in this damned rathole?"

"One thing you could do is keep the lights off. Anybody watching this place would wonder how they turn on when I'm not here."

"Personally I don't think anybody's watching this place anyway. I think you made it all up to keep me here."

"Keep you here? For what?"

"Sex, of course. Don't pretend you've never heard of it. Personally, I think you invented it."

"My, you're cute when you're angry. Actually, nobody is watching us at the moment, at least I don't think so, but there has been—the guy who shot your friend Ralph and left his gun behind. Remember?"

She shivered. "How do you know?"

"I saw him. And I've got news for you. He's got another gun—just like the one you saw, silencer and everything."

She shivered again and she wasn't frowning anymore. "He killed Glenna, didn't he?"

"That's my guess. Glenna and Ralph. And he's been looking for you. And," I said, "after today he's probably going to be looking for me, too."

She came close, staring up at me with big eyes. "Simon, I'm frightened."

"And well you should be. Which is why you're to sit still in this house and not do anything to let anybody know you're here. Do you understand?"

She nodded and tried to appear docile. I went into the living room and turned on the television. "Now," I said, "you can sit and watch that, or eat, or do whatever you want. But once I'm gone, don't touch anything. Don't turn off the set, don't turn off any lights. Go to bed when you want, but leave everything as is."

"What do you mean, once you're gone?"

"I have to go out for a while."

"And leave me here all alone? Who is she? Who've you got lined up?"

That's the trouble with sex kittens. It's almost impossible for them not to think about sex. "It's business," I said. "I have to see people."

"Monkey business."

I put a finger on her nose. "Listen, sugarpuss, if you ever want to get out of here, I've got to clear the decks. The police want you, the guy who killed Ralph wants you, and I've a hunch there are some other people who want you, too, but I haven't found out who they are yet. And I'm not going to find out if I stay home with you." I kissed her on the nose. "So you be a good girl and wait for papa and I'll be back when I can."

She didn't want to be a good girl. "Screw you," she said.

"I'd rather screw you," I answered, "but not right now."

"You can damned well bet not right now," she yelled, following me across the foyer. "It just might not be ever!"

I closed the door, made sure it was locked, and before I could start down the steps something large and fragile— like a lamp—crashed with a loud noise against the other side.

That's another problem with sex kittens. Sometimes they *do* get their minds off sex, and then what're you going to do?

11

THIS TIME there was no trouble at Marshall's massive gate.
The keeper, a different man from the last, took my name,
let me through and hurried to his little phone.

By night the mansion glowed with a warm homeyness.
You wouldn't think anything that big could look cozy and
inviting, but this place managed it. The sky was clear and
the moon was gleaming full and round just off one of the
turrets. The moon was white and cold, the windows amber
and warm, and the parking area off the driveway was
packed with a hundred cars. Sally had said there was going
to be a party. This looked like a mass gathering.

I left the heap on the grass off the driveway, hiked over to
the terrace and found the door half-open. Inside, in the
ample foyer with its naked stained-glass maidens, half a
dozen people, all with their coats on, were chatting in little
groups. They seemed casually at ease and it appeared,
since the evening was young, that they were coming, not
going.

I didn't know any of them and started to go by and
around. Then Sally Schyler appeared at the other entrance
and caught my eye. She was wearing a long flowing green
gown of reasonably fragile material that barely covered the
proper areas of her breasts and gave a view between them

that just excluded her navel. There was also a scarf that
somehow draped over one shoulder and the other arm, but
you hardly noticed that. It didn't stay in place and she spent
her time doing this and that with it, using it as a prop, the
way some people use cigarettes.

Then she was with me, pressing my hands in hers like an
opera diva welcoming a critic. "I was hoping you'd come,"
she said, drawing me along with her.

"You ought to stay out of that place," I said, referring to
the foyer with its open door and cold November air. "You'll
catch your death."

"You like my gown!" she said, reading between the lines.
"I wore it just for you."

That kind of stuff you have to shovel and I wasn't wearing my work gloves. I said, "Why aren't you mingling with
all those people with the overcoats on? I think they're
looking for direction."

"I only came for you," she said, hugging my arm against
her breast. "The gatekeeper said you'd arrived."

That's the way they do it in Schyler Mansion. You don't
have a majordomo collecting invitations at the ballroom
staircase and announcing the next arrival to the cast
below. The pronouncement is made from the gate so the
hungry lions have time to fight for the newcomer. I sensed
that Sally had plans for me not quite in keeping with my
purpose.

"This is all lovely, dear," I said, letting her snuggle my
arm, "but I do have to have a few words with your father."

"No problem," she assured me. "He's on the sidelines
watching the dancing."

"This is a dance?"

"Disco dancing. It's in the ballroom. And we're having a blast."

It was a blast. I could hear the music half a mile away. We went down long halls with constant breast contact mildly exciting us both, and finally we were at the ballroom. It was a vast arena with access through wide doorways, but entering it was like walking into a wall. That's how loud the sound was. I had to stay on the fringes for thirty seconds while my ears adjusted. Sally hung back with me, but her fingers were snapping and her feet moving and she kept waiting for me to be ready.

It was quite a scene. The ceiling was arched and painted twilight blue and looked as high as the sky. There were fluted columns all around, between which were doorways or high arched windows that gave a view of the lighted lawns and hedges outside. Tables and chairs edged the floor; the white damask tablecloths were cluttered with wineglasses, champagne bottles and trays of hors d'oeuvres—caviar, smoked salmon, jumbo shrimp, you name it. In the middle, a horde of at least two hundred people writhed, jumped, twisted and jerked in a frenzy to the massive sounds that blasted from the superduper speakers that were fed by the superduper electronically amplified instruments brandished on the podium at the far end. For those who love it, it was hedonic heaven, orgasm without the orgasm. For me, born into the wrong decade, it was bedlam.

I looked around for Marshall, but didn't find him. Instead Sally pulled me onto the floor into the midst of the throng, faced me and went into her thing. Her thing was something. I thought she was going to come out of her dress and now and then some of her did. I couldn't just stand and stare, though, so I made with a little gyrating and some this and that and wondered where I could get some cotton for my ears.

I have to admit, though, the music finally gets to you. It's like a drug in its own way, and I don't know if it's the way they pound home that beat or if it's the way the noise stops any other stimuli from getting through. Whatever it is, you end up thinking that, in all of the universe, this is all there is, and you begin to respond. All there is is rhythm, so you operate in rhythm.

Except that there's always that little corner of my mind that is watching what the rest of me is doing and stroking its chin and saying, "What made you think that...do that... feel that?" and I always have to answer to it, as to a guilty conscience. Like, "Well, it seemed like a good idea at the time," or "How did I know the gun was loaded?" or some such. Anyway, I always have to explain myself to myself, and out in the middle of the dance floor, with Sally writhing and gesticulating and showing off tempting bits of her anatomy, I was wondering why I was keeping pace with her and deciding that after all it wasn't her anatomy I was there to see, it was Marshall Schyler.

It took me a while, but I finally spotted him in a distant corner by the doors to the floodlit lawn. He was in shadow and as far away from the sound of music as he could get, but he was there, giving support to the social activities of his children or whatever it was that this disco thing was for.

The music continued without letup for so long I thought I was there for the night, but then the musicians had to stop to go to the bathroom or something and there was a pause.

I gave Sally's rear a quick goodbye pat and was gone before she had quite settled back on earth.

"Good evening, Marshall," I said, going to him with a glad-hand welcome without being sure he'd know who the hell I was. He did, though. He held out a hand to mine and his face was a broad grin. "Well, Simon! I'm so pleased you've accepted our hospitality. I saw you dancing with Sally. She's a most remarkable child, don't you agree?"

I agreed, except I wouldn't have called her a child. "Marshall," I said, "is there a place where we can talk?"

"Of course. You mean privately?"

The music was starting up again. "I mean where I can be heard."

He nodded toward the lawns outside. "How about there?"

I looked at him in his pristine dress shirt and elegantly lightweight tuxedo, the thin white shawl across his lap, and said I thought perhaps his study...?

"Nonsense, I'm no fainting lily." He inclined his head and out of the shadows came Mona. I hadn't even known she was there and that says something, for I don't usually get caught off guard and I almost never overlook pretty women. But there she was, coming away from the wall to attend to Marshall's needs. She was dressed in a black flowing gown with a black mantilla over her head, which partially explains why I didn't notice her, but she also had a young and beautiful face and all the desires that went with it. Her body swayed to the new beat that was served up by the five-man group at the front, but she did not go out on the floor dancing, she stayed in the shadows waiting to be needed. Well, if she ached to dance but had to be a wallflower, her life had other compensations.

She leaned over Marshall's shoulder and said, "What is it, darling?"

He indicated the doors. "Simon and I wish to go outside."

"Of course." She opened them and Marshall, manipulating his wheelchair buttons and steering handle, led the way.

"Ah," Marshall said, breathing deeply of the night air when we moved into its chill freshness. The moon blotted out all but the brightest stars, but those were sharp and clear. With the doors closed, the disco music was muted. Over the high hedges and trees glowed the lights of the Schyler mansion's garages. "I do love the smell of the night," Marshall continued. "I daresay you don't get the same delicious fragrance where you live down in the city?"

"There's a patch of woods around me," I said. "I do get a little more where I live than gasoline fumes and body odor."

"Then you are blessed," Marshall said. "For many of the people here tonight, this is their only escape from the slums of the city."

I said, "I noticed that the personnel on the dance floor were a cut below the jet-set crowd. What's this party all about?"

Marshall shrugged. "It's a fund raiser for a drug-rehabilitation center we're founding. You must have read about it. Most of the guests are contributors, the rest are reformed addicts. It's good for the contributors to see the kind of people they're trying to help—and what these former addicts have made of themselves. And, of course, it's the former addicts who'll staff the center."

"I have to say I didn't buy a ticket."

Marshall raised a hand. "Nor are you supposed to. You're an invited guest." He laughed and touched my sleeve. "You don't really think I'd put the arm on an invited guest?" He swung his chair around so his back was to the windows and he was looking at the hedges, the glow of the garage lights and the clear sky above. "What's on your mind, Simon? I know you're not here just for fun."

I made it short and sweet. I'd picked up the Lincoln he'd reported stolen and I'd picked up Jud Lorne, its driver. Jud had been staking out my condo; he'd been carrying a gun with a silencer, for which he had no license; and most important of all, he'd given Schyler Manor as his residence.

Marshall's mouth tightened and he shook his head. "I know," he said finally, "and I feel very bad."

"What does that mean?"

"I suppose you know that Jud has a criminal record?"

"No, but it comes as no surprise."

"He *was* a criminal. He's not a criminal now." Marshall cocked his head. "I see I have to explain. Schyler Enterprises, which is the name of the philanthropy that the Schyler fortune endows, is interested in rehabilitation, in restoring people who have fallen from grace to a worthwhile place in society. It is my belief—the foundation's belief—that this is a resource that is worth tapping. We can gain great benefit from the experience and contributions of people who have, shall we say, seen the other side of the coin." He looked up at me for approval. "How many of us have been there?" he asked. "They can tell us much."

If he wanted sympathy and understanding, I wasn't contributing. "What's this got to do with Jud Lorne and the stolen car?"

"I make it a practice," Marshall went on, "of hiring ex-criminals wherever and whenever I can. I don't put them in sensitive positions, of course. I don't give a thief the combination to the safe, for example." He wanted a laugh, but I gave him only a nod.

"But I believe," he went on, "not only in supplying money for the rehabilitation of lost souls, but in providing opportunity. As I just said, my drug-rehabilitation center will be staffed by former addicts. You ask about Jud Lorne. He's a criminal on parole. Do you know what a criminal has to have going for him to get out on parole?" Marshall waved a hand. "I don't mean 'good behavior.' The stupidest criminal in the world knows that unless he's in a tin-can jail he can pry his way out of, the fastest way to get free is to build up Brownie points as a model prisoner.

"What a criminal needs, besides that, is a patron—somebody who believes in him, who will take responsibility for him. In other words, society is going to want a fall guy. If the criminal jumps bail, for example, the society is going to collect from the bondsman. So I play fall guy for certain criminals who need a sponsor in order to get paroled." He laughed lightly—if his laugh could be called light. "It's my neck, Simon. I took Jud Lorne on as a garage mechanic to get him his parole, and if he fails me it's my head that's on the chopping block, not his. Do you understand my situation, Simon?"

I said yes, I understood it, but what about the stolen Lincoln? What about the gun he carried? What about his stakeout?

Marshall stared off at the hedges. "With all due respect to you, Simon," he said slowly, "there isn't much I can do about those matters."

"Come again?"

Marshall counted on his fingers. "First, there's the matter of the stolen car. As I explained to you yesterday, I ordered the car sold. Jud Lorne apparently had a particular feeling for that car and didn't want to see it go. He did not put it on the market as I'd ordered. Then, when you called this to my attention, I phoned the garage and demanded that the car be sold immediately. That's when he stole it— switching plates, would you believe, in order to hide his act. You caught him and turned him over to the authorities, and for this I am grateful. I can tell you that Jud Lorne is going to be put on probation because of this. If he does not shape himself up, I might just remand him back to the penitentiary."

I looked at this creep in the wheelchair. "You mean, if he promises to behave, you'll let him keep on working for you?"

"I'm not condoning the theft of the car, Simon," Marshall said, raising a calming hand. "But I have to understand the circumstances. Jud is particularly attached to that car—"

"The hell with this crap." I went around in front of the wheelchair and bent over Marshall. "Now you listen," I said. "Your pal Jud has been staking out my condominium, armed with a gun and silencer, while driving around in a car you've reported stolen, which carries plates belonging to another of your cars. I saw that car he drives leaving the scene immediately after Glenna Powers was shot by a gun with a silencer. Now what do you make of that?"

Marshall shook his head. "I think you misunderstand Jud Lorne. He was in the woods answering a call of nature when you attacked him. He wasn't watching your place. I have his oath on that. Besides, he had no reason to."

Marshall smiled innocently. "Why would anybody want to watch you? What would you be hiding?"

Then he tried to explain that Jud's stealing the Lincoln was a mistake, but not a serious one. Would I expect him to send the man back to prison for such a minor infraction?

I said, "The hell with Jud Lorne's oath. I'm telling you he wasn't answering any call of nature, he was staking out my place, and the spot he picked is littered with his cigarette butts to prove it."

Marshall lowered his head and squeezed his hands in his lap. "If that's true, I'm sorry. I didn't realize that. I believe he's reformed and is really trying—"

"He was carrying a .38 with a silencer. How do you define 'reformed'?"

"For that he's in trouble," Marshall admitted. "His parole may be revoked. This, of course, we won't know for a while—"

I eyed the son of a bitch. "Are you telling me that Jud Lorne is loose?"

Marshall's voice was very low. "Well, yes." Then he went on, "I posted bond for him. After all, I wouldn't press the stolen-car issue, so it was only the matter of his carrying a gun without a license. I think he's learned his lesson."

I said, "What about the murder charge? What are you talking about—he's learned his lesson?"

Marshall shook his head. "There isn't any murder charge."

"Listen, his gun—"

"Believe me, Simon, I've been in close contact with the police about this. Captain Perry Marstan, one of the high-ranking officials in the department, personally tested the gun and tells me there is no evidence that the gun Jud was carrying was involved in either of the recent killings."

I took a deep breath. "I see. So Jud Lorne is free now. He's out on bond?"

"I supplied the bond, yes. I have faith in Jud."

We went back into the ballroom after that. There wasn't anything else to talk about. That's the trouble with these damned bleeding-heart do-gooders: they really believe there's no such thing as a bad boy. All you have to do is fix up his environment a little and he'll do a hundred-and-eighty-degree turn. Marshall really seemed convinced that the hood who'd stolen his Lincoln and walked around with an assassin's gun under his arm was really the boy next door who got a little dog dirt on his shoe.

At least the conversation with Marshall was good for one thing. It told me that Jud Lorne wasn't behind bars in the city jail, something I might otherwise have assumed—with perhaps serious consequences. I had to figure the guy was gunning for me now just as much as he was gunning for Chelsea, which meant that the next time we met he might not be pretending to zip up his fly, he might be pulling out his gun. And it might be when I didn't know he was there.

The great ballroom was jumping with action, crashing with noise and trembling like the walls of Jericho, but I didn't notice. I was trying to put myself in Jud Lorne's shoes, figure where he was right that minute and why.

Then Sally was at my side, looking buxom and concerned. "Are you all right? What did father do to you?"

That's what she said, but in that disco den I could only see the movement of her lips. "What?"

She yelled, but it still did no good. I took her by the hand

and led her into the hall. I found a club room about half a
block down and closed the door. That way we could hear.
The lights were on and there were card tables set up, as if
for duplicate bridge, while chairs and couches lined the
walls. The room was empty, but it had recently been used:
the smell of pot was heavy in the air. "All right," Sally said,
trying to be motherly, "what did father do to you?"

Motherhood wasn't Sally's role, at least not yet, but she
did seem to care. "Your father," I said, "told me that some
hireling of his by the name of Jud Lorne is freely walking
the streets of our fair city."

Sally said, "I know Jud. Why shouldn't he be?"

"He's an ex-con, caught carrying a gun, which is about as
big a no-no as there is. Your father, unfortunately, regards it
on a par with littering."

"And you don't?"

"People who carry guns carry them for a reason. The
reason is to shoot other people. Otherwise people wouldn't
carry them."

"And you think Jud is going to shoot somebody?"

"I think he has, and will." I sniffed and changed the
subject. "Tell me, Sally, who's your supplier?"

She didn't get the drift and stared at me blankly. Sally
was long in some suits, but short in others.

"The drugs," I said. "Anything you want in Schyler Manor
you can have, isn't that right? You're a proper hostess,
aren't you? If the guest wants pot, or H, or cocaine, or angel
dust, you can provide it, can't you? It's good old Marshall
Schyler northern hospitality, isn't it?"

"You don't have to make fun of my father," Sally said,
offended.

I patted her arm. "No, no," I said. "I'm asking because I'm curious."

"You want something?" she said brightly. "No problem. Tell me your pleasure and I'll join you in it." Her eyes gleamed. "Opium pipes in my bedroom?"

I kissed her on the lips. "The trouble with that, sweetheart, is that if I were in your bedroom with you, I'd never get around to taking the first puff."

"We don't need the pipes at all, if that's what you mean."

It wasn't what I meant. It was awfully hard getting her to understand what I meant. "What happens," I asked her, "when you run out of opium?"

That wasn't a hard question. She said, "We get some more."

"That's right. But you don't get it at the corner drugstore. That's what I'm talking about. You have to buy it from somebody."

"Of course."

"Who's the somebody? That's what I'm curious about."

"Oh," Sally answered as if it were no secret, "a guy in town named Ralph Scorwitch."

12

UNFORTUNATELY, SALLY DIDN'T KNOW anything but the name. If anything was needed in the drug line, you dialed the number and asked for Ralph. She knew the number by heart and it was the right number—the one that was on the phone in Ralph's apartment.

"What if he wasn't in? Was there an answering service?"

She laughed at that. "If he wasn't in, you got no answer. You had to keep trying."

Where he lived, who he was, those were matters that hadn't bothered Sally. It was only important that the supplies be on hand.

"How did they get here?"

She didn't know and didn't care. "You sound like a detective."

"That's what I am."

"But this is a party. You're supposed to be on vacation."

"That's right. Let's go dance."

I went through some more of the disco with her and decided that hell isn't going to be filled with unbearable fire, it's going to be filled with unbearable noise.

I got away the next time the people making the noise had to go to the bathroom, and I swore I wouldn't go back again. I put Sally into the arms of a spaced-out zombie and went outdoors. Her mewing cries of complaint followed me, but I had to put my thoughts together.

Scorwitch provided the drugs for the Schyler family. Jud Lorne worked for the Schyler family. Jud Lorne had killed Ralph Scorwitch.

These were all assumptions, of course, comprised of Sally's word, established fact and my deductions. If I were right, and Jud *had* killed Scorwitch, the question was *why*. Had Marshall told him to? Had Jud some personal vendetta with Ralph? What would Ralph's death do to the Schyler family's drug supply, and who would want it that way?

I thought about the mansion's garages then. Their lights glowed above the trees. Activity was still going on there, at an hour long past a garage's usual closing time. Also, the garage was off limits to mansion guests, according to the mechanic who'd threatened me. So my problem was: where was Jud Lorne biding his time at this moment? He'd been one of Marshall's mechanics. He might have friends at the garage. He might have places to hide at the garage. A lot of interesting tidbits might be found at the garage.

The hedges and trees were no problem. I got through with hardly a scratch and found myself on a small slope with the garages and the mammoth apron just below. The amber arc lamps were bright enough for night football, but nobody was in sight. The cars were tucked away, the apron was clear and the only sound was the throb of disco behind me.

I went on down and looked into the first of the nine garage stalls. A car was bunked and sleeping. I tried the next and the next. The Chrysler wagon was in the third. That was the one that had borne the Lincoln's plates the day before. Now it carried the plates I had seen on the

Lincoln when I strong-armed Jud Lorne. That was an interesting switch.

I didn't get any farther because a voice behind me said, "All right, funny man, stick 'em up."

Like a damned fool I had underestimated the opposition. Or I didn't know there was opposition. In either case, the result was the same. I stuck 'em up.

The voice behind me said, "Frisk him, Harry," and a man appeared. He looked like another one of Marshall's parolees, meaning his face reminded me of a hatchet in a skull. He frisked me while the voice behind kept up a running monotone, calling me names and telling Hatchet where to look next. The voice didn't belong to Jud Lorne. Jud had a voice I wouldn't forget. This sounded more like, the mechanic I'd squabbled with the day before.

Hatchet found my gun, of course, and my wallet. He disappeared with the goodies and there were murmured comments behind me as the two of them counted their winnings. "So that's who he is," said Hatchet. "It figures," said the other.

I said, apropros of nothing, "I want to call my lawyer."

They brought me inside an empty stall with a lift in it. I didn't like the scene, but when the other guy's got a gun and you don't, you play ball. I turned for a look when we got in there and found the guy with the drop on me was the mechanic I'd thought he was. Hatchet swung a left to the side of my face and said, "Nobody told you to turn around."

I saw it coming, rode it and hooked him, left, right, left to the jaw, fast and hard. By hard, I mean I really put feeling into it. Guys like him bring out the ugly in me.

It wasn't a smart move, what with the tough mechanic

holding me in his sights, but sometimes I forget to be smart. So Hatchet went to his knees right where I could lay him flat with a right-footed dropkick, but the guy with the gun stopped me. He let off a shot a foot past my head and said, "The next one's not gonna miss."

I talk real tough when I've got nothing else going for me. I grabbed Hatchet by the collar and said to the mechanic, "You tell that to him, because if he lays another hand on me you're gonna have to aim better or I'll kill him."

Then I kicked Hatchet in the kisser as I'd planned to do, laid him out and put my hands on my head. "All right," I said to the guy with the gun, "whaddaya want?"

That's one of the tricks in this game. Most of these punks haven't been drilled in what to do when the routine stops being simple. The mechanic still had the gun, but he didn't have his number-one helper.

Then to top it off Sally Schyler's voice called, "Simon? Are you down there?" And it was coming closer.

The mechanic's eyes darted nervously and his hold on the gun grew uncertain. I yelled, "Come on down," in a big voice and was starting to feel real good. It's called over-confidence, and it's a mistake. I took a small step forward, lowering my hands as I did. The mechanic's darting eyes looked past me and focused. There was someone behind.

I tried to duck, but I was too late. Something that felt like a runaway tractor trailer hit me in the back of the head, and all the lights went out.

I SLOWLY BECAME CONSCIOUS of a throbbing pain. It was what woke me up. I cracked an eyelid and what there was to see was white, blurry and close. It hurt to look. I closed my eyes, waited and tried again. It still hurt, but I managed to take a survey. The white was pillowcase. I was in bed.

I didn't remember going to bed. In fact, I didn't remember what I last remembered, so I raised my head. A couple of inches was more than enough. The hammers started pounding my brain. It was a bed. I was under sheets and blankets, my head on a pillow.

I pulled a hand out from under the covers and it moved the way I wanted it to. Nice, obedient hand. I put it to my head and had it gently probe the terrain of my scalp. There were large lumps, sore spots and crusted blood near the back; the area was tender to the touch. But luckily I seemed to be all in one piece.

Now it began to come back: hatchet face, the mechanic with the gun, and somebody else, who had slugged me from behind. They'd meant business, the two that I saw and the one that I didn't. So why was I alive and breathing? Marshall Schyler's paroled criminals weren't the types to leave a job unfinished. Not the ones I'd met. And I was damned sure Marshall knew it. He wasn't paroling shoplifters and purse snatchers. He was employing the cream of the crop, the ones who'd be on death row if capital punishment came back.

I lifted my head again. Maybe it was a trick. Maybe I was in heaven. Or maybe they wanted to torture me first. There had to be some reason why I was waking up.

The room was an elegant bedchamber and it wasn't a guest room. It was used by someone—a female someone. The window curtains were frilly, the writing desk was fragile, the plants, the flowers, the design on the coverlet and the aroma all added their weight to the scales. I was in some woman's bedchamber. I can't say I was too surprised. Save for Marshall himself, the only people I'd met in his mansion were women. The only people who'd lift a finger for me were women. And Sally's voice had been the last sound I'd heard.

There are times when you feel rage and anger. There are times when you feel sick and helpless. There are times when you feel damned lucky to be alive. I was between two and three. Never mind the enemy. I wanted to hug a friend.

I looked around for a friend, but the room was empty. I didn't feel like it, but I sat up. You can't lie in bed when nobody's supporting you. You've got to get up and support yourself.

The first thing I discovered was that I wasn't wearing any clothes. And there weren't any clothes folded over any of the furniture in the room. That didn't set me on the road to recovery. If you really want to feel defenseless, try facing the world with no clothes on.

I threw back the covers and made myself stand up. It wasn't much of a chore. I fell down twice, but then I made it. After I had some balance I let go of the bedpost and wobbled to the closet. It had sliding doors and I fell down again. Eventually I got straightened out and took a look at what was inside. If I wanted to go in drag, I had my choice of costumes, but that was it. There wasn't anything but dresses to wear, not even a pair of slacks that might fit.

The bureau drawers told the same story. I felt like *Women's Wear Daily*.

I looked out the window. It was a twenty-foot drop to the frost-covered ground outside. I was looking two floors down into a covert courtyard, one of the many at Schyler

Manor, while a rising sun dismissed a fading moon, and a new day dawned.

I figured the hell with it and went back to bed.

WHEN I WOKE UP AGAIN the sun had swung to late afternoon and the rays were oblique. Most of the day was gone, but now at least my head didn't fall off when I sat up. My clothes were back, too, jacket and trousers cleaned and pressed, dangling on hangers from the bedpost. The rest of my things were in a package on a chair. By rest of my things I mean even including wallet, shoulder holster and gun. I went through the wallet and all the money was there. That was some guardian angel I had.

I dressed slowly, still trying to shake the ache in my head. It was only a dull throb now, but I knew it was there. I got my tie tied, my shoes and socks on, then picked up the phone by the bed and called my office. Eileen said, "Where have you been? Are you all right?"

I said I was, and what was going on?

"Captain Marstan called," she said. "The message is that he can't tell about the gun. It could be the same, but there's no way of telling. I don't know what he means, but that's what he said."

"That's all right, I understand it. Anything else?"

She gave me messages from a couple of clients and said, "Then there was a strange call. The man wouldn't leave his name. He only said he was a friend of Ralph's and if you wanted to talk to him, he'd be at Leone's Bar and Grill on First Street between eight and nine tonight, but you're to come alone."

"That's all?"

"That's all. I wouldn't go if I were you. I didn't like the sound of his voice."

"That's one helluva reason."

"But you probably will. I can tell by the way you laugh at me. Are you in trouble?"

"I don't know. Why?"

"Because I don't know where you are. I've been trying your home all day."

"Any answer?"

"Are you kidding? If I'd got an answer, I wouldn't be asking where you are. Where are you anyway, or am I not supposed to ask?"

"It's no secret," I said. "I'm at the Marshall Schyler residence at the top of Hilltop Drive."

"*The* Marshall Schyler residence?"

"*The* Marshall Schyler residence."

"Where've you been the rest of the time?"

"Same place. Ever since last night. It was a late party."

"She must be really something if you're only just now remembering you have an office."

"Fold up your little green-eyed monsters," I told her. "They have other ways of making you stay."

I said I'd see her the next morning and dialed the condo next, but like Eileen I got no answer. Either Chelsea wasn't playing the answering-service game anymore or something else was going on. I thought I'd better thank the guardian angel, pick up my car and drive down to the condo to find out.

The bedroom door opened and Sally came in. She was wearing an off-the-shoulder afternoon dress and looked very blond, very tanned and very attractive. "Well," she said, smiling at me deliciously, "you're up at last. How're you feeling?"

She was trying to be offhand and casual, but she was a mite breathless. She'd been hurrying, which meant she knew I was up, which meant somebody was monitoring the bedroom phone. I told her I thought I'd survive—thanks, obviously, to her good auspices. "Is this your room?"

She nodded. "I wanted you to be comfortable."

"What happened last night?"

"You fell against a steel beam and really made a mess of your head. Gus, the chief mechanic, was trying to revive you."

I felt my head. "Yeah, I see. Who else was there?"

"Joe Doxey and Harry Foyles. Why?"

"I just want to know whom to thank. Then what?"

"I had them carry you up here."

"With my gun and wallet and everything!" I was impressed.

"They'd taken those," Sally said with a shrug. "Their reputation isn't the best. I made them put them back."

"You're good. You really are."

"You just have to be firm with them. They're on parole, you know, and they have to behave."

"At least when people are watching. And they undressed me and put me—"

Sally laughed. "Don't be silly. Not they! Mona, Carla and I undressed you."

"That must have been fun."

"Of course it was fun. You don't think when we have a helpless male on our hands we aren't going to take advantage, do you?"

I agreed that I'd do the same if the positions were reversed and that I appreciated the refurbishing of my clothes.

"Well, you were lying on the cement and you had dust, dirt and blood all over you. We had to do something."

I said I was forever in her debt and made other goodbye noises. She started to flutter. "But you can't leave now. You're only just—you're still injured."

"I'll heal."

"Father's going to want to see you."

I said I'd be back, but I had business to attend to—things that couldn't be kept waiting. She went with me down the halls, telling me about the goodies on schedule for the rest of the day. She seemed to think the temptations would overwhelm me. That's the trouble with people who have that much money: they've never heard of responsibility. Temptation's the only weapon they've got.

13

ON MY WAY HOME I checked the parking area back of the shopping center, but there was no Lincoln. I swung around into the condominium and when I came up my little hill there was no rattletrap convertible, either. I hadn't known Chelsea had keys to the thing, but it looked as if she'd flown.

I opened up the condo and the inside was something. The lamp she had smashed against the door was scattered in the foyer, but that was only the beginning. In the kitchen half the crockery from my shelves was all over the tile floor. In the living room the table lamps lay on the rug, damaged but not broken. I tried the bedrooms. My bed was unmade and the pillow was on the floor; otherwise it was intact. All that was missing was any sign of Chelsea. She, her clothes, purse...everything she had was gone.

And where to?

I tried to phone her at her house, but there was no answer. I wasn't expecting there to be. She'd obviously left of her own accord, she hadn't been kidnapped; but the question was, where would she go and how far could she get? That car she was driving stood out like a hitchhiker's thumb, and it wouldn't be long before the cops—or Jud Lorne—had her.

I looked at the pad by the phone in case she'd left a phone number or the indentations of a phone number, but there was nothing. Well, she was of age, and I wasn't her keeper. She wasn't my problem, except that she didn't really know what the outside world was like. She thought it smelled of pot and felt like smack.

I called Perry Marstan and got him at his home. "Thanks for letting me know about the ballistics test," I said. "You think Lorne didn't kill Glenna?"

"I'm not saying that," Marstan answered. "I think there's a good chance—the kind of weapon and all. I'm only saying we can't prove it."

"So he's out on bond."

"That's not my doing."

"Having a gun on his person is in violation of parole. By rights he should be back in the pen."

"Like I say, it's not my doing. I just do what I'm told. Other people make policy."

"And you still looking for Chelsea Powers?"

"Yeah, why?"

"If you'll tell me what you want with her, I might have a tip for you."

"Are you trying to bargain with me, Simon? She's wanted, and if you know where she is—"

"I don't have any idea in the world where she is. Now do you want to tell me what you want with her?"

"Investigation leads us to believe she was in Ralph Scorwitch's apartment the night he was murdered."

"She's a suspect?"

"Or a witness. We want to talk to her."

"How'd you find out she was in Scorwitch's apartment?"

"We don't *know* that she was, we think she was. That's what we want to find out."

"For what it's worth," I said. "Glenna's car, the one she parked outside my door just before she got shot, is gone. I don't know if it got stolen or what, but if Chelsea had keys to it, she might be the one behind the wheel."

Marstan said, "Thanks, Simon. I'll have headquarters put out an all-points bulletin on it right away."

So much for that. I turned on the stove and put on some dinner, then got out the broom and dustpan and started cleaning up the mess.

I DROVE BY Leone's Bar and Grill at quarter of seven, taking it slow. If you know First Street at all, you know enough to stay away. It's not far from where Ralph Scorwitch got his lead funeral, and as I said, Jack McGuire and I grew up in the area—along with a bunch of other kids...some now dead, some serving time, a few who went on to bigger and better things. Leone's, though, was new. The neighborhood keeps changing.

There was a scattering of cars along the curbs on both sides, the streetlights were far apart and the houses crowded the sidewalks and each other. Leone's was a squat, dark, low-profile place, a remodeled and expanded first floor of a tenement flat. The building was near the corner, with a closed grocery store and boarded-up Laundromat finishing out the block. There was a lot of glass with a door in the middle on the street side of the bar. The name was over the door in pink neon script, with the same thing on a projecting sign. There was a green neon beer sign in one window, and a red one in the other. The lights in the bar and grill were so dim that the windows looked black.

I drove past to get the lay of the land, went around a couple of blocks and came back. I had no trouble picking the spot I wanted to park in. It was near the corner across the street from Leone's and had a clear view of the sidewalk in front of the cafe.

I got out, locked up and went down there. The door pulled left to right and opened between the bar and grill. The bar occupied the left half with room for tables and chairs against the windows. The grill was on the right and stretched down in back to a phone booth, the doors to the kitchen, and the guys' and dolls' closets. There were lights in both places, but they were so dim and so few that you thought you were wearing smoked glasses.

It was dinner hour and half the tables in the grill were filled, mostly with men, with here and there a fat wife, and nowhere any children. The menu was coleslaw, French fries and hamburgers with a beer chaser. The tables were bare, the floor was bathroom tile. I went to the phone booth and faked making a call for ten minutes. By then I knew all the faces in the place.

I went into the bar then, around the far corner, and had a five-minute beer. That gave me the lay of the bar side. I left without the bartender noticing. He was fat and bald and talked only to the established customers, who were glued to the seats in front of him.

It was ten after seven when I returned to the car and slouched down in the passenger's seat with my head below the raised seat back and my eyes just above dashboard level, giving me an eagle's-eye view of the cafe. Of course, I kept the windows up and doors locked.

My headache was gone. Aspirin and a good belt of Scotch had taken care of that. Now I felt ready and willing, gun in holster, all senses on the qui vive, and that tense, exhilarated feeling in my stomach. Somebody was trying to set me up for something—somebody who knew or suspected that I was involved in the Ralph Scorwitch thing. And who might that be?

Meanwhile the cars went by and a few people passed. They were the ones to watch. They weren't your friendly next-door neighbor; they were on the prowl. Friendly next-door neighbors stay off the streets at night in this part of town. I watched and memorized the cars and people, but mostly I watched the front door of Leone's.

More came out than went in and I scratched the ones who left. The newcomers I did a quick run-through on. I was too far away to get a good make on their faces, but that didn't matter. Their clothes, their way of handling themselves were just as identifying. I paid special attention to those who showed up around half-past seven. I pegged that as the most likely docking time for whoever had phoned Eileen.

Time hung heavy, and I thought about what the hell I was doing there. I wasn't on hire. I wasn't doing this for money or for fun. I didn't like the setup, but I didn't have to attend the party. Nobody had said, "Be there, or else!" I didn't have any mystery to solve or bones to lay to rest. As far as I was concerned, Jud Lorne had blasted Ralph and had staked out Glenna's home because Chelsea had been a witness. I showed up instead of Chelsea, so he staked me out and killed Glenna by mistake. Since then he'd staked me out still thinking I'd lead him to Chelsea.

Now that Chelsea was gone, Jud was on the loose and hungering for my own guts as well as hers. And somebody had made an anonymous phone call to Eileen that had "trap" written all over it. And what was I doing? I was arming myself to walk into the trap.

Why the hell wasn't I going to a movie somewhere? Why the hell wasn't I back with Sally Schyler finding out the rules of the games she played?

You can drive yourself bananas if you try to think too much. A little self-insight might keep you from tripping over the curb, but too much and you're apt to fly out of belfries.

At quarter-past eight I took a deep breath, felt the comforting grip of my gun one last time and got out of the car. It was time to find out what the future held in store. I didn't think anybody was watching me. They'd have had to be lying low longer than I had, and the hoods I've known are short of patience. Like Jud Lorne having to smoke cigarettes in the woods. You can outwait 'em every time. So that's one of my trump cards, but you have to remember they have a few aces up their own sleeves.

No one was on the street when I made my move. I meant it to be that way. I crossed the between street, went past the boarded-up Laundromat and the grocery store with its one little dangling light back near the freezing compartment, and wandered in the front door of Leone's Bar and Grill. There were half a dozen people at the bar, and two of the tables were occupied. In the grill section they were still doing business, but only a third of what they'd been doing before. The guys out this way eat early.

I headed into the bar, but made a big enough entrance so I could be seen from the grill. I didn't worry about being overlooked, though. The boys around here don't make that kind of mistake.

In the bar I took my old spot around the corner where I had a view of all the action, meaning the front door, the long sidewalk windows and everyone in the bar. It was a corner and my back was against the wall, but that way nobody could sneak up behind me.

I ordered another beer and nursed it through three cigarettes. I don't smoke much anymore, except when I'm nervous, and maybe I'm not as patient as I'm trying to make you think. Anyway, better smoke on my breath than booze. If anything came up for grabs, I didn't want to go for it with my reflexes all sloshed.

At twenty of nine I had another beer and felt self-conscious. The glasses were so small you could die of thirst at my consumption rate, and people might think I wasn't treating myself right. I was supposed to be out for a good time, not waiting for my fate, but after all my talk about patience I was the one getting edgy. Was I being outwaited and manipulated? Halfway through the second beer I decided that would be it. Either I was being stood up, or I was playing against the first team. Whichever it was, it wouldn't be to my advantage to hang around.

Then a man came in from the grill. He had macho shoulders—at least his sports jacket did—and wore a loose raincoat. He had salt-and-pepper hair and a lazy, inquiring manner, like someone who can't see very well.

He didn't do any faking, any edging nearer, any accidental-type stuff such as, "Sorry to bump you," or "Oh, I didn't know you were there."

He came right to me and said, "Mr. Kaye, my name is Manny Floyd."

I kept my right hand wrapped around my glass. "Hello, Mr. Floyd." I was meeting his gaze, reading his eyes, showing I was paying attention, but I was also watching the others in the room, seeing who noticed, who didn't, and who didn't notice enough. Macho Man was one of those who'd come in at half-past seven, in the company of a tall, reedy type with unkept black hair and an unconscious habit of touching the left side of his foreign-correspondent trench coat to make sure his gun wasn't lost. Right now, though, there was only Macho Man. Foreign Correspondent wasn't in sight.

"You're wondering why I called you," Manny Floyd said, aiming a finger at my chest like a .45 and smiling as if reading minds was his business.

"That's right, Mr. Floyd."

"Manny's the name. Call me Manny." He looked around. "Let's find a place where we can be private."

He wanted to take me away from my lookout point. "Whaddaya mean?" I said. "This is as private as you can get." I gestured to the bar stool next to mine. "Keep your voice low and even the bartender would have to lean over to hear us."

He couldn't afford to push so he took the seat, but he didn't like it. It looked like the minor leagues, his giving in so fast and showing his disappointment in the bargain. But never underestimate an opponent is my motto. That's when second-raters knock off champs. He signaled the bartender, who was taking an order half the bar's length away from us.

"Well, I'll ease your curiosity, old chum," he said, and

gave me a friendly nudge. "Curiosity killed the cat. Ya know that, dontcha? And I don't want anything like that to happen to you."

"Thanks, old chum."

He leaned closer and whispered, "It's about the Glenna Powers-Ralph Scorwitch killings."

That was interesting, his linking the two together. "What about them?"

"I gotta tell you," he said, leaning forward again, his eyes more serious now, more searching. "Glenna was killed by mistake." Silence hung while he waited for a response.

I said, "If she was, why are you telling me?"

"She was killed on your steps."

That was supposed to explain everything. "Go on."

He dropped his voice so low I had to lean forward myself. "You know who killed her?"

I shook my head.

"Y'ever know a guy name of Jud Lorne?"

This was no time to feign ignorance. I was being evaluated. "We've crossed paths," I said.

Manny Floyd was satisfied with the answer. He gave a slight affirming nod and put a hand on my arm. "Stay away from Jud Lorne. He's poison."

"You mean he shot Glenna?"

He nodded somberly and turned as the bartender came for his order.

14

MANNY INSISTED on buying a round and killed off a boilermaker as if he was going for the *Guinness Book of World Records.* I had another beer and didn't try to compete. "It was a mistake," Manny repeated. "Jud was gunning for Glenna's sister. I guess you didn't know that."

He was being interestingly frank, so I thought I'd explore. "What about Ralph Scorwitch?"

"He's the reason Jud was gunning for Glenna's sister— girl by the name of Chelsea Powers. Ever come across her?"

"I've heard the cops want to talk to her. What's your interest?"

"Chelsea and I are engaged."

I kept a poker face, but only just. He was throwing some wicked curves. "You and Chelsea?"

"That's right, old chum. Now you see why I'm interested?"

"I see why you're interested, but you haven't told me why this Jud Lorne's gunning for her."

"He blew down Ralph Scorwitch. Whaddaya think?"

"And?"

"And Chelsea saw him do it. Ya get the picture?"

I let the light come into my baby browns. That lighted his.

I sipped my beer and waited. He was telling the story the way I had it pegged. That established his credibility—except for that "engagement" business. He'd have to run that past me slower and better.

He didn't. He put a hand on my sleeve and he was looking troubled. "That's what's bad," he said. "Jud's gunning for my baby, and I don't know how to protect her."

"Have you reported him to the police?"

He looked at me. Then he laughed mirthlessly. "So I finger him to the cops. I got no evidence. And he's got connections. He got pulled in yesterday afternoon on parole violation and he's out on bond. There ain't no way the cops can lay a hand on him. They can't save my Chelsea."

"Rumor has it she's blown town. Maybe she doesn't need saving."

"You don't know Jud. He's relentless."

Manny waited a long moment. Then he looked over at me and gave a quick nod. "I shouldn't be saying this," he said out of the corner of his mouth, "but she hasn't flown the coop. She's still in town."

"Where?"

He shook his head. "I'll show ya, but I won't tell ya."

"How do you know she's there?"

"She called me this afternoon."

"How long's she been there?"

Manny shook his head. "No idea," he said.

So, had Chelsea quit my place, gone to some other pad and S.O.S.'d her boyfriend? I asked, "Is she safe?"

He shook his head morosely. "She's a goddamned sitting duck," he told me. "Jud's homing in, but I don't know how to get her outta there." He turned. "That's why I thought of you."

"Whaddaya mean, why?"

"You're a detective. Chelsea's sister was killed on your steps. You got ins, you got connections, you got know-how. I ain't got nothing. Jud's after Chelsea and I can't go up against him without help." He looked me in the eye. "I want you to help me get Chelsea away safe."

"In other words," I said, making sure the eye contact was good, "you want to hire me as a bodyguard?"

Manny thought for a moment, then nodded vigorously. "Yeah, yeah. That's what I want." He pulled a fat wallet out of his hip pocket and opened it. "What's the tab, Simon? What d'ya need?"

Apparently free escort service wasn't one of his angles. I held out my hand. "Let's say two hundred to start."

The wallet diminished not at all in size as he peeled off and pushed four fifties into my hand. I'd estimate he had better than a grand left.

He got off his stool to stuff the wallet back on his hip, then got back on to order another round. I asked, "What for?"

"To celebrate," he said.

The bartender poured and served, and out of nowhere Foreign Correspondent appeared in the entryway going out the front door. I pretended the new beer tasted flat and pushed it aside.

The setup was simple. Any sucker would fall for it. Manny Lloyd's girl friend, Chelsea Powers, was hiding out from the guy who wanted to kill her. Motive: she'd watched him kill someone else and he wanted to keep her from tattling. My part in this arrangement—what I was supposed to do for the two hundred dollars I'd been paid—was to help Manny get Chelsea out of the spot where she was hiding and into some new spot. Two hundred bucks for moving a girl from here to there. And Manny would lead the way. All I had to do was be there, maybe cover the rear, maybe give moral support, maybe hold the girl's hand. (It was diamonds to daffodils Manny had no idea I'd done a good deal more than hold Chelsea's hand.)

There were, of course, a few small catches—nothing big, mind you. We walked out of the bar and up to Manny's car, a big chrome job as gaudy as his sports coat, and I wanted to know where we were taking this Chelsea girl once we rescued her from Jud Lorne's searchlight eyes. He didn't have a place in mind. Well, let's say he didn't have a hideout in mind. We could take her to his pad. That, he decided, was the thing to do. And what if Jud Lorne...?

We didn't have to worry about that, Manny insisted. Jud didn't know where he lived. That was the kind of answer that makes you glad you've oiled your gun.

Manny drove through dark streets over to the deserted part of town down near the wharves where there's nothing but broken pavement, broken warehouses and boarded-up tenements. If my part of town is bad, you should see this. The cops pick a corpse a week out of the gutters and they only go in there in pairs.

The looming hulls of freighters filled two of the piers. They carried scattered lights topside but were dark otherwise. The arc lamps along the road threw a blue glow, but the shadows were deep. Great, dark warehouses, blinking with broken windows, stared emptily.

Manny drove by the harbor docks slowly. "She's around here someplace."

I said, "She's got good taste."

He glanced at me warily, the minor leaguer trying to handle the ball cleanly. He turned down a side street, past the loading platforms and storage depots for the fish and vegetable markets, past Cutler's Bar, a dive that reputedly has a trapdoor dump into the harbor, which serves as both an escape hatch and a graveyard shuttle.

Manny pulled in at the curb half a block farther along. Only three other cars were in sight parked on different sides of different streets. Except for a man slouched on the steps of an abandoned flat four houses up, no one was in sight. It's an area of town I don't ride herd on, and when I came around the side of the car my antennae were waving like hula hoops. Manny, however, pocketed the car keys and slammed the door like a homecoming businessman ready to welcome his dog. He gave not a glance to the dingy, threatening deserted flat in front of us, but mounted the steps, pushed open the door and went inside.

I followed and he produced a small pocket flashlight with a bright beam and let it explore the interior. There were stairs at the back and he nodded. "Up there," he said.

"She's up there?" I tried not to sound too surprised.

He nodded and led the way. I followed behind, and from the way the stairs creaked I thought the roof would fall in. Manny was busy playing leader so I slipped my gun from holster to jacket pocket and kept my hand on the grip. I'm not quite as big a fool as Manny seemed to think.

From the second floor we went to the third floor, then down a hall to a door at the end. There was a big chalked X on the panels and Manny paused to point. "See," he whispered.

"She's there?"

He nodded and led me to it. He pocketed his flashlight and pulled the door open slowly. The room was out of view to the left and was lighted by a flickering candle. Ahead was bare floor and the facing window. "Here's where she is," Manny whispered, and tried to usher me in.

I braced my feet and caught his wrists. "You first," I muttered, and gave him a shove. In he went, stumbling and at the same time shouting. The shouting was drowned out in what sounded like a preinvasion bombardment. One of the weapons was a machine gun and it cut loose with its identifying staccato rhythm. Interspersed, and playing counterpoint, was a one-two-three, low-voltage hissing sound. And in front of the display, Manny Floyd twisted and turned as the bullets belted him, looking like a drunk disco dancer sinking in a sea of booze. He screamed as the guns let go, and his features were twisted and taut. Then he went into his dance and his mouth hung slack, his eyes turned blank and his knees folded slowly.

The guns stopped before he hit the floor. Too late the trigger fingers let go. They'd "offed" one of their own, and shocked silence followed.

Manny fell down with his tongue hanging out, and footfalls sounded. The guy with the chatter gun came into view. It was Foreign Correspondent, in full trench coat regalia, gun cradled in the crook of his arm, and the expression on his face registered disbelief, chagrin, astonishment and horror.

That was nothing, however, to what it registered when he looked up and saw me in the doorway. It turned into

disbelief, chagrin, astonishment and horror squared. Like
Manny, he was a minor leaguer, and in that one moment he
knew it, and he knew he'd die there.

I squeezed two lazy shots at him while the look was still
on his face, before the adrenaline could start pumping. I
don't mean I was lazy, I mean the shots were lazy. I
snapped them off like target practice, when nobody's going
to interfere and you've got time to aim.

I carry a .38 and .38 slugs pack a wallop. They may not
blast holes like a .45, but they'll knock you over. This pair
hit Trench Coat three inches apart and one inch above his
chest button.

They knocked him against the opposite wall, they made
him drop his machine gun, and they left him with the same
disbelieving look on his face.

It was the kind of sight that distracts a man's attention. I
mean, if you're in a small room with a buddy and buddy boy
takes a couple of fatals straddling his sternum, it's hard not
to watch his death dance. This is what I counted on, and
when Trench Coat went back against the wall, I came in the
door. Trench Coat wasn't playing the game alone. That's
not the way it's done, and besides, there were those
whisper shots hissing under the hot-and-heavies that
Trench Coat had been dealing.

It was what I thought. Jud Lorne was there, gun and
silencer in his hand, beside the table with the candle, which
was the only furniture in the room.

He wasn't ready for me, but he was quick. He was staring
at Trench Coat sliding down the wall into his grave, but he
caught the movement when my gun and head appeared.
His gun hand swiped the candle and he dived at Trench
Coat.

It was so fast that I hesitated. I'm telling you about distracting attention, and he distracted me. My eye followed the candle, and he was in his dive when the room went dark.

I fired a shot at where I figured he should be, but I was aiming into a black hole. Two whipping whispers from his silencer responded and they took pieces out of the wall too close to my head. Jud Lorne was no second-rate assassin.

I backed out of the room a step and held. There was nothing to hear, not even breathing. The opposite window began to appear, dark gray against the black. I felt the wall with my free hand and guided myself along the hall two more steps and went down on one knee. If Lorne came after me, he'd be outlined against the window and I'd be ready.

There was still nothing to hear. I did a crab step backward and a board creaked. I needed to get around the corner to the stairs. If someone threw on some lights, I had no place to hide.

I worked it in stages: step, step, listen; step, step, listen; and always keep watching the window.

When I was around the corner I breathed again. I also found out how much I'd been sweating. My underwear felt like a wet bathing suit and my trousers were clinging.

I waited a couple of minutes with my head around the corner still watching that distant window, but there was only the same old silence. Maybe I'd nailed him. Maybe those two shots he'd snapped off were his last words on the subject. Maybe I was soaking my clothes for nothing. That, however, was something somebody else could find out about. I only wanted out.

I crept down the stairs as quietly as possible, made it

through the front door and took a great, deep breath of the fetid, rancid outside air. It smelled like attar of roses.

Around me the street was the way I'd left it—empty. Except, of course, for the three parked cars—four, counting Manny's —and the derelict slouched on the steps a few doors down. There'd been shots, but nothing had changed. In this stench-ridden part of town the sound of bullets was swallowed up by the night.

I looked around and frowned. I'd taken the trip with Manny and run all these risks in the expectation of learning something—mainly what had happened to Chelsea, but maybe a few other things as well; such as who had dropped the anchor on Ralph Scorwitch, and why. But all I'd learned was that Manny had set me up for Trench Coat and Lorne, and I didn't even know what rock he'd crawled out from under.

His car was still there, though, and I climbed in and went through it, stuffing everything in the glove compartment into my pockets, taking along anything else that was loose.

I got out and slammed the door. The derelict was still on the steps. The house with the two or three bodies was dark and still. I moved away from there, keeping the car between me and the house. I didn't want Jud Lorne sniping at me from the windows.

When I got around the corner I moved fast, trotting to the next corner, zigzagging from there for three more blocks till I was clear of the area. Then I headed for the populated streets, called the police with an anonymous tip from a street-side phone booth, hired a taxi to take me back to my car and headed for home and a shower.

15

IT WAS AFTER THE SHOWER, with a hefty Scotch beside me on the kitchen table, that I went through the loot from Manny's glove compartment. The car registration listed a better address than you'd expect for someone that stupid. I'm not saying he wasn't clever, I'm saying he wasn't smart. So, with little brains but a big address, he had to be illegit. That much was obvious. But it also had to be a large operation, and he was well up the ladder.

It was drugs, of course.

Everything in the case was related to drugs. The drugs game is the biggest thing going. It's so big you can't touch it. The profits are so enormous they'll turn the feet of a saint to clay. And Manny was in it—up to his eyeballs. So were Jud Lorne and Trench Coat. Most crooks were in it, and the bleeding hearts like Marshall Schyler only make it easier for them to set up their operations. I wondered how much Marshall knew of what was going on. Was he an ignorant jerk? Maybe he winked at the drug traffic and thought it was cutesy-poo. Maybe he had a hand in it. Maybe that wheelchair got him around more than you'd think.

I put the registration aside. Manny's house might need investigating.

Among the rest of the stuff there was only one thing of

note. It was a small wrinkled flier that had been rammed into the glove compartment and that gave the address of a disco den. The flier was complete with come-ons about the bands and the quality of music; then, in the asides, it indicated to the cognoscenti what else was available in the areas far from the dance floor. You really want to dance? They had the floor and the band. The rest of the place was sex and drugs.

It was named Nero's Nest, and it sounded interesting. I don't mean because of the way the flier painted it, which was tarnished gilt with the lead showing through. I mean because it wasn't advertised in the local dailies, a la the massage parlors and the porno films, and because I'd never heard of the place before—and my ear's set pretty firmly to the ground.

The evening was still young and I was thinking about an early bedtime, but this flier was like a diamond to a gold-digging blonde. It was all the rejuvenation I needed.

I went up to the bedroom, took off my terry-cloth robe, dressed in fresh clothes and was out and on the road before twelve. The dive—pardon me, disco joint—was eleven miles outside the city limits, out near the border of the next town, out where farms and fields still existed and specialty houses (like this one) were plunked down in the middle of virgin territory. The territory was about all that was virgin.

The building itself looked like a roadhouse, one of those dine-and-dance ensembles that were popular back when gasoline didn't require mortgage payments. If the building was not overly large, the parking area was geared for a shopping center. Let's face it: whatever the cost, sex, booze and drugs are here to stay.

It wasn't really late in disco language, so I didn't have to park more than a hundred yards away. The main door was heavy and needed two hands. Inside, there was a large red-carpeted lobby with a velvet restraining rope and a two-hundred-and-fifty-pound bouncer to unhook it. He wore a tuxedo, but it didn't make any difference: you knew he wore wrestling trunks underneath.

He wanted to see my wallet when I came in. I showed it to him and said I didn't know they were head counting celebrities. He grunted something that sounded like "oink," let me through and motioned to the stairs.

I went up and the sound that came down reminded me that I'd forgotten cotton for my ears. I cursed, went up for a look around, saw nothing but the scene I'd run through at the Schylers': screeching noise, heavy beat, frenzied people and not an unlonely face in the crowd. It was bedlam in Bedlam and just as alien. I circled the floor twice and there wasn't a face I knew.

Okay, that meant down to the depths, down to where the action was.

That part wasn't so easy. Only the dance floor is on limits. The rest is off, and guarded, and passage to it is made difficult. In the first place, you don't know where the doors are. In the second place, if you find them, they don't open. In the third place, if you get through, you're going to run into some more two-hundred-and-fifty-pound bouncers who're going to want to see your wallet. And you'd better be carrying certain cue cards in there or the next door you take will be into the parking lot.

It took me a while, but I found the right routes and I had a gilt-edged credential with me to get by the guards. It was Manny's car registration. Manny's name was on it and the name was magic. All the down-below doors opened and the dungeons became accessible, and I expected Satan to be greeting me at the last door and showing me the furnace.

Inside the last door it was hot and smoky, but it wasn't a furnace. The smoke was pot smoke, and the heat was something pseudosauna, geared to encourage the removal of clothes. And a helluva lot of clothes removal had been going on.

. The room was large and low ceilinged. The walls were black, the decor red. There was a heated swimming pool in the center, illuminated by red underwater floods. The smoke was so thick you could get high just breathing. The background noise was diluted disco from upstairs.

The clothing of the customers, almost without exception, was pelt—dripping pelt, as a matter of fact—something that might strike the newcomer with interest, but which struck the stoned inhabitants not at all. They wandered around in naked innocence, like latter-day Adams and Eves, and they couldn't have cared less, nor known about it less. They smoked their tight-packed pot cigarettes, they sweated like wet towels, and they had the animation of underfed zombies. Well, you have to go through this world one way or another. This was another.

I held my breath as much as possible and peered through the smoke as much as possible. I didn't know what I was looking for, and I didn't know what I'd find. All I knew was that the way my clothes were starting to dampen, I'd soon be stripping till I was as naked as the rest. The atmosphere encouraged that sort of familiarity.

And then, there she was—Chelsea Powers—over near the edge of the pool, bathed in its ruddy glow. It was by her body rather than her face that I knew her. I had to get closer to identify the face, but the body was something I'd come to recognize. It was that facet of her that was most on display.

I went over to her. She was listlessly dipping one foot in the water over the side of the pool. Then she saw me and started to dive.

I caught her wrist and steadied her. She tried to pull away, but she isn't the strong type. The best her struggles could do was make her breasts quiver. "I hate you!"

"How'd you know about this place?"

"Let me go, you—"

The "Let me go" part was pretty trite. The rest of what she said was very imaginative.

I thrust her arm behind her back and pulled her up close. "Sweetheart," I said, "I care about you. You're up for grabs. You know that, don't you?"

"You think you're going to get me back to your lousy flat?" She didn't say "lousy." She had much choicer, X-rated epithets, but we'll play it low-keyed.

I kissed her. "It may not be heaven," I said, "but it's better than hell."

As I said, I'm not all the great lover I'd like you to think. The kiss landed on her like sawdust and she spat it away. She had a few more X-rated things to say, the gist of which was that I should get lost. Obviously I'd have to study up on kissing.

The temptation was strong to bow with gentlemanly chill, remark upon the pleasure of having made her acquaintance and get the hell out where I could breathe air instead of burning weeds, and sweat water instead of peyote.

Nevertheless, this kid wasn't out of the woods—at least by my map. I don't know what map she was reading, and I needed to pack her away in mothballs again, at least until I found out what had happened to Jud Lorne.

Chelsea didn't like being interrupted when she was into her own thing. She put two fingers of her free hand into her mouth and gave a shrill whistle.

That brought a couple of gorillas to the fore. They were clothed in sweat suits, complete with underarm and crotch stains and with some dampness showing through from the creases around their bellies.

They didn't waste any time. One hit me a ponderous belt to the kidney, which made me let go of Chelsea. The other shoved her out of the way so he could sink an arm like an I beam into my gut. She did a neat, casual dive into the water. It was something I noted just before the pile-driver arm blacked me out.

I was being hustled through halls and up stairs. I flailed with my arms where I could, and when I did I caught another pile driver in some soft, vulnerable part of my anatomy. The griping part of it was that they were eviscerating me and I wasn't even denting them.

I thought when they threw me out onto the gravel of the parking lot that that was the end of it; I'd be able to put the pieces together and spend a couple of days in bed.

No way. They had their tie-ins and I was no sooner in the open air than there blinked the blue-flashing lights of a police car. From nowhere, there appeared a tuxedoed man with dark hair and beard, reflecting dark glasses and a voice like corn husks. He muttered words to the cops and gestured angrily at me. Troublemakers at Nero's Nest were removed on the double by city-paid men in blue, and that meant that Nero's Nest had the approval of the powers that be. And that meant a lot of things, not all of them pretty.

Uniformed men took me from the sweat-suit brigade, tumbled me into the back seat of the cruiser, said an obsequious, "Goodbye, Mr. David," to the tuxedoed Galahad in black beard and silver glasses, switched on the sirens and alarms that go with the blue lights, squealed around in a tight circle and took off down the highway for town. They were uniformed, but that didn't mean a thing. For one thing, I didn't recognize them, nor they me. For another, they didn't do even a routine search, and there I was in their back seat with my gun in my holster—oiled and reloaded—and they thought I was some helpless acidhead. Our local police force has certain lacks, but no authentic member of the force is that stupid.

I rode it out with them, getting my head rescrewed and some of the aches out of my body where the gorillas had strong-armed me. If they took me to headquarters I'd play dumb. If they took me someplace else I'd stick my gun in their ear.

IT WAS ALL on the up-and-up. They belonged to the auxiliary police force and they really did take me to headquarters. At the desk they tried to tell Sergeant Nick Grady that I'd been drunk and disorderly at Nero's. Nick wasn't listening. He was staring at me and pressing the button to Perry Marstan's office. "There's a warrant out for you," he said. "Sorry, but that's the way it is."

"You mean for this business at Nero's?"

"No."

Then Perry appeared and I said, "Don't you ever go home?"

That wasn't the right opening on this occasion, for all he

did was shake his head and look haggard. "Where'ya been?"

The auxiliaries who brought me in told him I'd been at Nero's, but he waved them away. "You can call off the watch," he told Nick, which meant they'd been staking out my condo waiting for me to show.

I figured they must have tied me to the shoot-out down by the docks, but I was damned if I knew how. They had a ballistics record of my gun and they might have been able to match the slugs I put into Trench Coat, but that would take a couple of days. In any case, I played dumb and said, "What's this all about?"

"You don't have a glimmer?" Marstan was looking very solemn.

I shook my head.

"What've you been doing tonight?" he asked.

"Why? What's happened?"

"Never mind, just give us a rundown."

So it was like that. The thing about cops is they never tell you anything, they make you tell them. Except that I play the same game, so conversation can get pretty boring. "Never mind the rundown," I said, "what'm I supposed to have done?" (That's what I mean about boring.)

The auxiliaries explained again that I was at Nero's, but Perry still wanted something better. "Let's go in the office," he said, beckoning.

I followed and closed the door and leaned against it. "You got the tape running or do you want a stenographer? Either way, we'll have to wait for my lawyer."

"It doesn't have to be like that," Perry answered, getting behind his desk. "There's no point in waking up your lawyer."

"I wonder about that," I said. "The atmosphere around here isn't very friendly. I get the distinct impression I'm supposed to have done something naughty."

"Nobody's accusing you of anything, Simon."

"Except you're down here making like I'm the reason you aren't home with the wife and kiddies. Who called you out on a night like this, and what for?"

He tried again. "You don't want to talk it out, just the two of us—off the record?"

"Talk about what?"

He gave in first. "About a little shoot-out down in the dock area about half-past nine this evening."

I took a chair and lighted a cigarette, which, as I've said, I do when I want to appear casual. "Anybody hurt?"

Perry flattened his hands on the desk and stared at his fingernails. "I think you know the answer to that one."

"Oh, for Christ's sake," I exploded. "Stop the mumbo jumbo. Somebody got shot down around the docks tonight and for some reason you think I did it. Did the guy who got shot point a finger, or do you have some hard evidence placing me at the scene?"

"It wasn't one person," Perry said, "it was three people."

"Oh, now I shot three people? Are they all dead?"

"They're all dead."

"I sure am hell with a gun. Three against one, huh? Did they have any weapons?"

"They were all armed. Two had their guns out, one didn't."

"Where was this?"

"A deserted house on Bellows Street."

"What was I doing there, besides killing three men?"

"That's what we'd like to know."

"You know what it sounds like?" I said. "It sounds like a trap. Three guys are lying in wait, and in I go and against superhuman odds I blast them. I'm not only super good, I'm super dumb."

"That's not quite the way we read the picture," Perry answered. "Guy number one, the mug with the gun on his hip, was machine-gunned by guy number two. He might also have taken a couple of shots from guy number three, who had a gun with a silencer—"

"That lets me off the hook," I said. "I don't own a machine gun."

"I said guy number two killed him. But guy number two took two slugs in the chest from a .38—"

"You've recovered them already?" I said with an overdose of admiration, because I knew the autopsy couldn't be held before the morning. "That's pretty fast work."

He knew he couldn't fool me on that one and he hedged. "We estimate them as being from a .38," he amended.

"Oh," I said dryly. "For a minute there I thought you were going to say ballistics had traced them to my gun."

He didn't like my sarcasm and he didn't like not being able to nail me to the scene. And that was what was funny, because he still hadn't shown any reason why I should be a suspect.

"No," he said. "We'll have to wait for ballistics. If," he grumbled, "they can make anything out of what we've got."

He'd given it away and I couldn't help smiling. He was saying the bullets I'd put into Trench Coat had come out the back and fragmented against the walls. Marstan was fishing. He had nothing.

"So, go on."

"The way we read it," Marstan continued, watching me cannily, "is that guy number one, a man named Manny Floyd—you know him?"

I shook my head.

"Manny, we figure, was leading another party into a trap, but something went wrong and Manny got shot instead of the other party." He looked at me. "That make sense?"

"I don't know Manny. It depends upon how dumb he was."

"Or how smart the other party was."

"Oh," I said, giving it the old upbeat inflection. "Now I get the message. The police department figures only a smart guy could have backfired their trap. And since I'm the only smart guy in town, naturally—"

"I didn't say that," Marstan growled. "All I'm saying is that, from the layout, we get certain pictures as to what happened."

"All right, what else happened?"

"What else happened is that this certain party who put two slugs into guy number two's chest then swung his gun and put three more slugs into guy number three."

"Guy number three is the one with the silencer?"

"That's right. And his name was Jud Lorne." Perry sat back and clasped his hands behind his head as if waiting for me to confess.

"Jud Lorne is dead?" I was thinking of Chelsea.

"That's right, and you and he—"

I stood up slowly and leaned over the desk. "Are you telling me that you and this whole goddamned police force have picked me as your prize suspect because I've had a quarrel with Jud Lorne?" I held out my hand. "Gimme your phone. I'm going to sic my lawyer on you like you've never seen before—"

That forced Perry's hand. "Well, it's not only that," he said, waving me away.

I put my hands on my hips. "What else have you got, and don't tell me bullet holes that just might possibly have come from a .38."

"No, no, it's more than that." He tried to reestablish control. "Manny Floyd," he announced, "was carrying your phone number in his pocket."

"And what other phone numbers?"

"No other phone numbers."

"And that's your evidence? It smells like a plant." I reached for the phone again.

Perry pushed his hands at me placatingly. "Now look, Simon, I didn't say we're charging you with anything. We only want to talk to you, find out what you know about these people. Somebody killed two of them—self-defense without a doubt. All we want to do is clear up the details."

All cops are the same, even if they're supposed to be friends. Since he'd have to turn me loose, I didn't fight him for the phone. But he should've known better in the first place. I had been a cop, too, before I went into private practice.

"All right," I said, "those are your details. What else have you got on me? And I mean something that says they didn't all shoot each other!"

Perry shook his head. "There was an outside party involved," he said. "That party rifled the glove compartment of Manny Floyd's car. The car was parked nearby and the compartment was empty. We figure that happened after the shoot-out, meaning somebody walked away from the three bodies when it was all over."

"Was that somebody trailing blood?"

A quick look came into Perry's eyes. "No."

"Too bad he didn't get nicked because I'm not carrying any wounds."

Perry looked me in the eye. "You know something, Simon? No matter what you say, I have a hunch it was you."

"That and a fire hydrant will buy you a parking ticket."

"You still don't want to tell me your alibi for tonight?"

"Only when I'm in court. Are you holding me or am I free to go?"

Perry sighed. "Get the hell home, will you?"

He sounded real sorry he couldn't nail me. Some friend.

16

I WALKED OUT of Perry's office and the timing was nifty, for coming in the front door of the precinct, with a cop on each arm, was Chelsea. What's more, she was dressed. (With other girls you take that for granted, but with Chelsea you have to specify.) The clothes were the ones she'd worn to my condo—and how many days ago was that?

Well, Jud Lorne and the cops had been hunting for her for a long time. At least it was the cops who'd got her. If she talked, though, she could put me into a bucket of fever. Perry wouldn't like my not turning her in.

I tried to read what was in her heart, but she played it like two icebergs passing in the night, and I was left with nothing to do but go home to bed and ponder my fate.

That wasn't all I pondered. I lay flat on my back with the light on and a pack of those cigarettes I almost never smoke at my elbow, and I stared at the curtained window opposite the foot of the bed and did some heavy thinking. The gist of it was that I was being played for a patsy. Jud Lorne hadn't set me up for the slaughter with the help of Manny Floyd and his trench-coated friend. Jud Lorne might have wanted to slow-kill me over an open fire, but somebody else had made the arrangements. He was the scheduled executioner, but he wasn't paying for the party.

Somebody had put him up to it and when he bungled the job, that somebody had pumped three bullets into him to keep him quiet. Someone had come into that house after I left to find out what had gone wrong. And the timing had to have been close, for the cops would have been on the scene within minutes of my anonymous tip.

That meant someone had been watching the show. Someone saw Lorne and the trench-coated guy enter the house to take up their positions. That someone saw Manny and me arrive and follow suit. That someone would have heard the shots and would have seen me come out again, seen me rifle Manny's car and take off. That someone knew who I was and that something had gone wrong. And if that someone had then tipped the cops, that would explain Perry Marstan's conviction that I was involved. It wasn't a phone number in Manny's pocket that put him on my scent, it was a tip from an eyewitness. And who was the eyewitness?

I'm not smart enough to be a really good detective. If I were, I would have paid attention to that "derelict" sitting on the steps four houses down, pretending to be in a stupor. Live and learn, they say; except that if I don't learn a little faster, I'm not going to live very long.

So, if I was figuring it right, Jud Lorne hadn't been my only enemy. I was a monkey wrench is somebody else's plans. The trouble was, I didn't know whose machinery I was messing up.

I lighted another cigarette to ponder that one. It's not good for your peace of mind to know someone's sighting along a gun barrel at you and not know what duck blind he's aiming out of. There are two ways to play that game. One is to run like hell and never come back; the other is to figure out whose finger is on the trigger and cement him in a cemetery before he can open fire.

The first option is chicken, the second is foolhardy. I chose the second, but not because I'd rather get shot than lay eggs. It's just that there's no way I can run. I've got clients, I've got Eileen, the office, the condo, my life's savings. My whole lifetime is here. The hell with starting all over when I'm almost thirty years old. Starting from scratch is for kids.

So I have to stand and fight. That means learning a helluva lot in a helluva short time; and where to begin?

I spent a long time kicking things around, testing and discarding various options, suspecting and unsuspecting this person and that.

So I was still awake when, at half-past three, the doorbell rang.

Who the hell would be coming by at that hour? You guessed it: Chelsea.

She was standing impatiently on the enclosed stoop at the top of the stairs when I switched the light on and cracked the door an inch on its chain. I'd already seen her car outside, but I still had my gun at the ready. It's best to know from nothing.

I let her in and she shed her coat in the foyer and threw it at a chair. I said, "Hello, Miss Iceberg, where did you come from?"

She wasn't inclined to be playful. She went into the kitchen and undid her dress.

I followed and tried again. "I don't like to sound like a suspicious husband, but where have you been and why are you here?"

She peeled the dress off, throwing it on the table, and all

she had on were her shoes and her pants. She kicked the shoes against the icebox.

The hell with the sweet talk. I got real tough. I said things like, "Whaddaya think you're doing?" and "What were you doing at Nero's?" and "What'd you tell the cops?"

She grabbed my hands and rubbed them over her breasts. "Shut up, you bastard," she said, "I wanna get laid."

"Then why don't you go back to Nero's—"

That kind of comeback was a waste. As I've said before, she can do things to you that make you perform a hundred-and-fifty percent better than you thought you could. When she's got her mind on sex, no matter how hard you try, you aren't going to be able to think of anything else.

She didn't even have to pull off her pants.

I did.

"WHAT'D YOU TELL the cops?"

"Huh?"

"Rise and shine, sweetheart, it's time to talk straight. What'd you tell the cops? I want it blow by blow."

"G'way."

I pulled the covers off of her. "Do you want coffee, a slap in the face or a walk around the room?"

"Lemme sleep."

This was Chelsea and me at seven o'clock the next morning. I wasn't much after two hours of sleep, but she was nothing at all. Seven A.M. was more like bedtime to her. I don't think she'd got up at that hour since she stopped teething.

It was mean of me, routing her out of bed like that, but if you're going to twist somebody's arm, you might as well catch him when he's weak. And Chelsea's arm needed twisting. She was sitting on information I had to have, and I figured this was the time to pump her.

I dragged her to her feet and went on at her about the police. She tried to struggle, but she was too weak. She tried to rest her head against my shoulder, but I twisted her away and forced her to walk to make her talk.

"I didn't tell the cops anything," she said desperately. "Please, can I sit on the bed?"

"Are you going to be a good girl?"

"Haven't I been a good girl?"

"Will you get your mind out of the hay? We're talking about the police. Or at least we're *going* to talk about the police."

She kept trying to put her head on my shoulder, but I wouldn't let her. "I don't think you're very nice," she complained, "after all we've been to each other."

"I promise to turn into a candy-coated bonbon just as soon as you've said your piece."

"I'll talk," she promised, "if you just let me sit down."

I told her she was going to stand until she'd said enough to earn the rest. I walked her around the room two more times to prove it and threatened her with a trip down to the kitchen for coffee. That sobered her. She was so groggy she was afraid of the stairs.

Bit by bit I got the story out of her. It took a mile and a half of walking because I had to cross-check and double-check her every statement, for she'd lie to me anytime she thought I'd believe her.

The gist of it was that Nero's Nest was the place where Ralph Scorwitch had held his great orgies and it was the one place, besides my own pad, where Chelsea would be accepted.

Who threw the parties now that Ralph Scorwitch was dead?

Chelsea didn't know. The drugs, the drinks and the sex were free. Why would she worry about where it all came from? The sex, of course, came from her, but she didn't regard it as a contribution; that was part of the fun.

"Everybody wins," I said.

"That's life. Can I go to sleep now?"

"In a little while. Why did the cops arrest you? What did Captain Marstan talk to you about?"

"He wanted to know who killed Ralph."

"What did you tell him?"

She said wearily, "I told him what I saw."

"How did he know you were at the scene?"

"I dunno."

"Who let you into Nero's Nest last night?"

"I just walked in."

"Come on, come on," I said. "Who do you know there, now that Ralph's dead?"

She said she didn't know anybody, but I kept after her. I wanted to know whom she was protecting, and why. She kept begging to go to bed and I kept saying first she had to answer questions.

What finally came out was that a man named Patsy Million was her contact, that he'd been a friend of Ralph's, that she'd met him at some of Ralph's parties, that Ralph had told her Patsy was the one to call if he was tied up.

When I finally let her go back to sleep it was almost nine o'clock. She could really wear a guy down. Meanwhile, she was back in dreamland before she hit the pillow.

I threw the covers over her pretty little slumbering body and went through her purse. The only clue to Patsy was a phone number. His name and address weren't in the phone book, but I found the number listed under Nero's Nest.

It sounded like his place of business. Since it seemed that the guy who'd killed Lorne would soon be coming for me, it also sounded as if Patsy was the man to see.

But first I needed to recoup and regroup. I called Eileen and briefed her on my plans, then set the alarm for noon, climbed into bed beside Chelsea and conked out almost as fast as she had.

17

THREE HOURS OF SLEEP, a shower, a bite of lunch and I felt like a new man, ready to brave the lion's den armed with my trusty gun and my iron nerve. To tell the truth, I had butterflies in my stomach. I wanted to stay away from Nero's Nest in the worst way. It was enemy territory, I didn't know the layout and I didn't know how many sweat-suited punks had the run of the place. Nor did I know how much artillery they carried. I was Theseus going after the Minotaur without knowing what the hell it was. Bad as that deal was, it beat sitting around waiting to be ambushed. Better to go after him even if you don't know who he is. If I went to Nero's Nest I might find out.

I left Chelsea sleeping, and Eileen with the address, boarded my heap and was off to the races. On the way I tried to remember if my insurance was paid up and my will was properly filed: the Degases and the Rembrandts go to my mother, Eileen gets my fishing pole and my chess books.

It didn't take long. The lone, squat building gloomed through the barren trees, and when I turned onto the "In" driveway and hit the parking lot, all I could think of was airport runways flanking a terminal.

The runways were empty except for a few cars parked

close by the service entrance. I stuck my buggy in with the others and tried the service-entrance door. That was the one they hadn't locked, and I went through a hallway to storage rooms and the kitchen. A couple of unshaven, farm-team football types were scrubbing out caldrons. They looked as if they could have used the caldrons for teething rings. Nero's Nest didn't seem to employ anyone who couldn't bench-press Godzilla.

I looked in on the duo and said, in tones to match their size, "Where the hell do I find Patsy Million?"

One of the gunkos looked up and nodded toward the front of the lodge. "Try his office. Up the stairs behind the counter."

I waved him a thank-you and he put his head back inside the caldron. The pair of them looked as casual as I acted.

So it was on to the front part of the pavilion and up the stairs behind the check-in desk. There were two rooms with open doors up there, both giving view through wide windows onto miles and miles of highway left and right. If Armageddon approached, Patsy Million and his friends would be the first to know.

The second room was living quarters, but I didn't get that far. The office came first and it was occupied. Behind the desk was the man with the beard and dark glasses I'd met the night before, the one who had thrown me to the gendarmes, the one they called Mr. David.

I didn't like Mr. David. I don't like people who turn you over to the cops without giving you a chance to explain yourself. I don't like people who allow big ugly bouncers to beat up nice little people like me. But mainly I don't like people who wear mirror-type dark glasses, outdoors or in.

That's one of the tip-offs that you're in bad company—
when the creep hides his eyes.

Even without seeing his eyes I could tell by the way he
froze that he recognized me. I didn't waste time with him. I
went in and said, "Where's Patsy?"

"Patsy?"

The hell with that crap. I went into the living quarters
next door. There was a living room and that was as far as I
got before the creep came in behind me. I was expecting
that, and he wasn't. I was waiting beside the door and
wrenched his arm behind his back. I said, "Do you want to
talk, or do you want to hear the bones crack?"

He went to his knees, shrieking in pain, and I drew the
arm up another notch to warn him against any more noise.
He was quiet then, but he was very white of face. That's the
way I liked it. "Where's Patsy Million?" I said. "I asked you
that before."

"Please," the man said in his hoarse voice, "he ain't
here."

"Let's go find out." I brought him to his feet and pushed
him ahead of me. We started into the suite and a door
slammed at the other end. Patsy had big ears.

I marched Mr. David through all the rooms of the upper
quarters, but Patsy Million had gone down the back stairs.
Back in the front room I threw Mr. David onto the couch.
"All right, what's he afraid of?"

Mr. David cringed. He looked ready to wet his pants, and
I wasn't coming on all that tough. "I don't know," he
croaked. "Honest, I swear to God."

"Who's your supplier?"

"Supplier?"

There was that crafty note in his question. He wasn't

scared enough to spill his guts—not yet. I took out my gun and showed it to him. "Drugs, my friend. Where does he get them? Who does he pay hush money to? Who does he report to? Who's above him on the totem pole?"

"I don't know," the man blubbered. "I swear I don't know."

I pointed my gun at him. "How'd you like me to knock off one of your ears?"

If possible, he turned even whiter, and he came off the couch onto his knees, his hands clasped in prayer. "Please, please have mercy."

I was standing in line with the door, of course, and I caught the flicker of one of Million's hoods coming around the top of the stairs. He ducked back, but I knew we had company.

I grabbed the praying mantis by the collar and yanked him to his feet as a shield. The time had come to get out of there—that is, if I could.

He yelped and screamed when I marched him ahead of me into the hall. "Don't shoot, don't shoot," he was screaming so the hoods in the place wouldn't start random firing around corners.

When we reached the end of the hall, the stairs below were empty. The watchdogs had either backed off or been called off. I went down the flight with my gun in David's back, announcing in a loud voice, "If anybody so much as shows a face, this yellow bastard gets it through the spine."

There was no sound in the place, no sign that it wasn't deserted. I marched Yellow Belly out the front door and around to my car in the back, and all he did was cry and sob and beg his cohorts not to make a move.

When I opened the door to my car I gave him a kick in the

ass that sprawled him on his face, wrecking his glasses, tearing the knees of his trousers, scraping his hands and offending his dignity. I like to think I'm a kindhearted guy, the type of person mothers beg their daughters to marry, but cowards stick in my craw, especially cowards who enter high-risk occupations.

I slammed my car into gear and only barely resisted the temptation to run my wheels over the sonuvabitch. I put tire marks on the flap of his coat instead.

I ARRIVED AT THE OFFICE in a big peeve. Eileen said, "At least you're home safe. I don't think you're smart going to places like that alone."

"I never claimed to be smart."

She patted my brow, kissed my cheek, sat me down in her chair and said, there, there, she'd get me a cup of coffee.

"Lace it with brandy."

"My, you are in a stew. You ought to count your blessings."

"What the hell am I blessed about? I risked my life and I come back with absolutely nothing. I could have stayed home and watched TV."

"Like hell, the commercials would bore you. At least you were getting some exercise."

She put a mug of coffee in front me. I said, "The brandy's in the file drawer under *B*."

She kissed me on the forehead. "I know where the brandy is, and the gin and the rye and the Scotch."

"And don't kiss me on the forehead. You're not my mother. If you're going to kiss me, kiss me where it counts."

"Aha," she said and swung her hips. "Sex is rearing its

ugly head again. I think the patient is recovering." She went into my office and got the brandy. "How much?" she said, pulling the cork and holding the bottle over the mug.

"Lots."

She poured to the brim and put the bottle aside. "All right," she said, "what were you supposed to find out that you didn't find?"

"I'm looking for Mr. Big of the drug racket in this area."

"So are the F.B.I. and the local cops and various assorted other agencies. What made you think you could succeed?"

"I can twist arms more freely than they can."

"And why are you so hot on the trail? Who's hired you? I don't seem to have any record or any retainer."

I patted her derriere and she moved away. That was a little too familiar, at least for this afternoon. As I said, we walk a tightrope, she and I. "Always thinking of the pocketbook," I said. "Always worrying about the rent being paid."

"Always worrying about my salary being paid," she said. "And what are you worrying about?"

"I'm worrying about who's setting me up for execution. It's somebody big enough to own Jud Lorne and a number of other like properties, as well. It's somebody who thinks I'm getting close to him, and I don't know why he should think so."

"How about Marshall Schyler? He's big. He's got enough money to buy anybody, and Jud Lorne worked for him."

"I've thought of him, but he's trapped in a wheelchair and I don't think he can wield that much power from that kind of confinement. It's possible, of course, but it doesn't seem likely."

"But who else has that kind of money?"

"Anybody running the drug racket has that kind of money. The trick is not to let the money show."

"Do you have anybody in mind?"

I shook my head. "The only name I've got is Patsy Million. If I can make him bleed a little he'll name the next guy up the ladder. Then I'll go after him and get the next name. It's a little slow, especially when they hide behind their bodyguards. Meanwhile, Mr. Big is trying to stop me in his own way."

Eileen sat down in the visitor's chair, looking pale right down to the bottom of her cleavage. "Simon," she said, "get out of it. It's not worth what can happen to you."

I took a big slug of coffee and almost choked on the brandy. "I wish I could," I said, "but I can't just run an ad saying I won't chase them anymore. They're going to keep on until they get me, which means I've got to keep going in self-defense."

She looked at me. "This is the first time I've ever wished you weren't a detective."

"Think about the bright side. Lots of cases are interesting and challenging and need my personal attention—like right now. How do we stand on what's open?"

"The files are on your desk," she said and took a big slug of my coffee herself. She shivered as I had and put the mug down. "Now I know why you shouldn't drink on the job."

That was that for a while. I went into my office, thumbed through the open cases I was supposed to be working on, and decided there was no way I could concentrate on things where my hide wasn't involved.

At five-thirty Eileen brought in a batch of papers for me

to read, approve and sign. I asked, hadn't she gone home yet? She said no, she hadn't.

I went over the items while she took notes, and the phone rang. It was for me, she said, with her hand over the mouthpiece. "Mona Schyler."

That made the hairs on the back of my neck prickle. I took the phone and sat back, putting a cheerful note in my voice while Eileen watched me narrowly. The moment she detects a youthful-sounding female voice on the wire she gets cat's eyes. You can't call her jealous because after all she's only my secretary and I've never laid a hand on her except for the safe spots. So it may be a maternal complex, the good shepherdess looking after the little black lamb in the flock. In any case, that's for the Freudians to worry about. I had more immediate irons in the fire—like what would Mona Schyler be calling me for?

"Hello, Mrs. Schyler," I said in my best-bib-and-tucker tone.

Her own voice was lilting. "Oh, please, Simon," she said. "You must call me Mona. I thought I'd made that clear the other day."

"What can I do for you, Mona?" I asked, keeping up the gung ho good cheer while Eileen's eyes spat daggers.

Mona had a problem.

What kind of a problem?

She couldn't go into it over the phone, but it was imperative that she see me at once. Could I come to Schyler Manor right away?

"It's a little past closing time," I said, trying to evaluate what new situation I might be falling prey to. "Is this a business or pleasure call?"

"I didn't know detectives had closing times," she answered lightly. "What will get you here, business or pleasure? It could be either, but if I know you, I should say 'business.' But I can't tell you over the phone. You will come, won't you—as soon as possible?"

I nodded. It was one way to stay close to the action. "I'll be there."

"Good. I'll be in the drawing room."

I put down the phone and looked into Eileen's green eyes. "Mrs. Schyler," I said, "wants to discuss business with me—in the *drawing room*."

"You may call her Mona, I don't mind."

"Mona wants to discuss business—"

"In the drawing room. I heard that. With Mr. Schyler?"

"She didn't say."

"How old is Mona?"

"About my age."

"She sounded more like my age."

"She matures gracefully."

18

I WENT HOME for a quick change of clothes and a shower. I wanted to wash away the grime of Nero's Nest. Chelsea was as I'd left her, lights out and hardly breathing. Sex, sleep and hallucinogens were all she needed. I hardly recall her touching food. I left her a note saying I didn't know when I'd been back but she should eat something and be a good girl. I didn't ask her not to break up any more furniture lest it give her ideas.

Then I shoved the heap into gear and headed for Schyler Manor and Mona and whatever that was going to bring.

The guard at the gate gave me a wave. He was getting to know my car. I felt like Louis B. Mayer driving through the gates at M.G.M.

I left the car at the terrace and the front door was open with the green-liveried butler waiting to welcome me. I told him I was supposed to report to the drawing room and he nodded knowingly.

Mona was by the windows looking out at the lighted courtyard, wearing a loose-fitting muumuu that hugged her hips but was shapeless everywhere else. The effect, I have to tell you, was more alluring than you might think. Add to that the sensuous way she moved, the fact that the unzipped front of the gown was an open V down to her waist with no sign of undergarments, and it's hard not to get ideas. In fact, it's hard to believe you're not supposed to get ideas. Girls don't usually wear come-ons if they mean, "Stay away."

I looked around when she turned, but there was no mistaking it—we were alone. "I'm glad you could come," she said, moving toward me, offering both hands. I clasped them and backed off a half step so she wouldn't bump into me. Her perfume wasn't any easier on the blood pressure than the gown she wore. The way it gaped, she was showing off more than she should, but I doubt it was more than she meant. Women are very alert to such things, no matter how innocent they may appear.

I said, "Where's Marshall?" Partly it was to make sure he wasn't lurking in the shadows, and partly to remind her she was married.

"Oh," she said, dismissing him, "he's with parole people going over things about Jud Lorne. He was killed last night."

"I heard."

"It was some kind of a gunfight and he wasn't supposed to carry guns. He was a parolee, you know, and there's quite a to-do."

"Especially with Marshall putting up bond for him."

"Oh, did he do that?"

"So I'm told." I was still holding her hands and trying not to look down the gap in her dress. "You wanted to see me? Your message made it sound urgent. I came as soon as I could."

She nodded, then took my arm and warmed it against her breast as she led me to the door. "We'll talk about it in private," she told me. She took me up three flights in the elevator, then down a hall and up a flight of curving steps to a room in one of the towers. All the while she kept up idle conversation and hugged my arm against her. That was Sally's tactic and it had the same effect. By the time we were in the elevator I could feel her nipple rubbing my sleeve through her muumuu. She was working herself up and letting me know it. One part of me was enjoying it, but the other part was saying, "How come?" and wondering what the catch was.

The tower room was circular, twelve feet in diameter, with a double bed, a couple of chairs, bureau, clothes closet and bath, plus windows looking out on the terrace in front and over the trees to the garage area on the side. It was hot up there and she pushed open the front window. By now she'd let go of me, but she waited for me to join her. "It's a lovely view from here," she said, "but the room does get awfully hot." I came alongside and she shook her muumuu by its gape to circulate some air around her body and make sure I could see where the air went.

I'm not a prude and I don't claim many scruples, but I do try to keep my hands off other men's wives. Even so, I can tell you I wanted to take her in my arms in the worst way. My throat was dry and it wasn't just the heat, it was plain honest-to-God lust.

I backed off from that window and looked out the other. Gus, the head mechanic, was out on the apron tuning up a car. That reminded me that he was someone I owed a beating to and it got my mind off Mona for a little.

She came up behind me, slid a hand down my back and

over my rear end. "Sit down," she said and took my hand, drawing me to the bed.

She sat languidly, but I stayed on my feet. "I think I'd better understand what I'm here for," I said. "I gather it's not business, but pleasure."

"If you insist, we can make it a business arrangement," she pouted.

"Why me?"

She rose again, took my hands and pressed them to the gap in her gown. "Because," she said, very softly, "I felt something when I showed you around the other day, and I sensed that you felt the same thing. I attracted you. I know I did. I don't make mistakes about things like that." She pushed my hands inside the gap.

I almost let them roam. Girls are hard for me to resist. I swallowed and freed myself. "Aren't you forgetting you've got a husband?"

"No," she said, shaking her head. "That's something I never forget. You must realize he can do nothing for me. He's crippled. He is incapable of being a husband."

"But you married him anyway. There's something in it for you."

Mona made a face of distaste. "You are trying to make it dirty—that I married him for his money. It's true that he's rich, but I also love him. You can love someone even if you cannot have sex with him."

"So you get the sex on the side?"

She came close and unzipped the front of her gown another foot. "He knows I'm human," she said, and pulled the gown wide so that it fell from her shoulders. "He wants me to be satisfied."

She was offering herself, and what she had to offer was

hard to take my eyes from. I didn't try. "So why didn't he call me in and tell me?" I said, looking at all the things a gentleman shouldn't look at.

"The choice is mine, after all. And who wants to talk about it? I'm not something to be bartered over. If two people want to do something, they do it." She let the muumuu fall to the floor.

"And your husband approves?"

"I wouldn't do it if he didn't," she whispered.

"Then why are we up in this hothouse tower? It wouldn't be because it's got steps, would it, and Marshall can't climb them in his wheelchair?"

"No," she said, "it's because this is the hottest, sexiest, most isolated room in the house. All you have to do is give yourself up to it." She took my hands and pressed them against her breasts, and tilted her face up for my kiss.

That hands-to-the-breast business was one of Chelsea's tricks. I was meeting a lot of eager-beaver broads these days. It's enough to make you suspicious. I don't mean Mona wasn't ready and willing. I don't mean she didn't want it as much as I did—right now. But she couldn't have been that hot and avid back when she phoned to set up the deal.

What she was doing here in the tower might be off-the-top-of-her-head stuff, but the phone call had been part of a plan. And the plan was what bothered me. I had the feeling that I was being set up, that I was being duped by the oldest gag in the books—throw the beastly male a winsome broad and you can shear off his locks, read his secret papers, rob him, kill him, enslave him, use him however you please.

And here was this luscious, lithesome female trying to compromise me and making me ache to be compromised. Something clicked in my mind and I suffered a sudden loss of interest. All that mattered was that I get the hell out of there fast.

I moved her aside, gave her a quick kiss on the lips and said, "Thanks, but my lines are busy. Maybe a raincheck, if you're giving them out?" I left her and headed around the bed for the door.

Mona gave a little yelp. "Not yet," she said, and hurried to the bureau.

I wasn't waiting. I threw open the door and there, as much startled as I, stood Marshall Schyler with a snub-nosed revolver in his hand.

He was wearing a Band-Aid over his eyebrow and another on his cheek; the hand that held the gun had a Band-Aid on the palm and the other hand was bandaged. The gun was small, a .32 at the most, and the man himself was so taken aback that he couldn't move. That was good, because I could.

I snatched the gun from him with my left hand and karate chopped him with the right. There wasn't room and I couldn't get leverage, but I hit him hard enough to let him know I was up and about, and then I threw him into the room. I know it sounds as if I was rough on him, his being a friend and all, but guns make me nervous. I tend to forget my good upbringing.

He stumbled into the bedpost, tripped over his feet, and went flat on his hands and face in front of his very naked wife who was standing by a bureau drawer that was almost as wide open as her mouth. I, of course, had his gun.

Something about the way he stumbled had a familiar look and suddenly all the pieces tumbled into place. When they did, my mouth was almost as wide as Mona's. I swung the door shut, stepped over the guy and grabbed him by the collar. He was on his hands and knees and I jerked him to his feet. He stumbled back against the doorjamb and it gave his head a whack. He was awkward, all right, just the way he had been when I booted his tail into the parking lot at Nero's Nest. The Band-Aids on his face were because of his broken mirror glasses, the ones on his hands from scraping them on the gravel.

"Some cripple," I said, going to the other side of the bed and holding the gun on him. I turned to Mona. She was smoothing her hands on her thighs, and her face was haggard. "So he can't make love to you! Was that his idea as the way for you to seduce me while he waited outside for the proper moment to kill me and claim it was a crime of passion?"

She didn't answer, and she didn't meet my eye.

I turned to Marshall. "And you! You're quite a master of disguises. The paralytic wheelchair victim one day, Patsy Million's assistant the next. Is that how you keep watch on your empire? Is that how you monitor the drug trade? You didn't want Patsy to talk to me, did you? You were afraid I'd make him betray you. And I would. I'd get to him in time. That's why you made Mona get me out here to seduce me so fast. You didn't dare take a chance.

"And what other disguises do you use? Let me guess. How about a derelict sitting on a doorstep down by the docks last night, watching me walk into your little trap with Manny Floyd? Did you hear all the shooting? And when it was I who walked away after it was over, you had to go see what happened, didn't you? Jud Lorne was alive up there. Only Jud knew too much." I looked at the gun in my hand. "How about it, Marshall? You think the bullets in this gun would match the ones they took out of Jud's body this morning?"

Marshall's eyes were darting. He wet his lips, and then he looked at Mona and shrieked, "For Christ's sake, kill him! What're you waiting for? Kill him!"

I turned. There'd been a gun in that bureau drawer Mona had opened; a big black gun. Mona had it aimed at me, holding it steadily in both hands.

I should have wondered what she had been looking for. I should have done a lot of things. That's the trouble with people who have no clothes on. You get to feeling they're helpless.

"Come on!" Marshall screamed. "Pull the trigger, pull the trigger!"

I didn't swing my gun her way or she would have. All I could do was talk. "Don't do it," I said. "You don't want to do murder. He makes you whore for him now. What will he make you do if you kill for him? He'll not only own your body, he'll own your soul."

"Kill him!" Marshall shrieked again. "If you don't it's the end! It's the end for both of us!"

"It's the end no matter what happens," I said to her. "Him and his parolees! He uses them the way he uses you. He sent Jud Lorne to kill Ralph Scorwitch. Ralph was getting too big for his britches. That was it, wasn't it? Then Glenna Powers. Then he tried for Chelsea and for me. Now he wants you to do his dirty work. Don't do it, Mona. The walls are falling down. Get out of here alive!"

Marshall pointed a finger at her. "You pull that trigger or I'll have you killed! You hear me?"

Then the door opened beside him and Sally came rushing in, saying, "Father, what the hell is it? I could hear you in my room!"

She saw me and my gun and stopped. She saw Mona and her gun and staggered.

Marshall was fast enough this time. He grabbed Sally as a shield and in a flash had a penknife out of his pocket and against her side. She shrieked and struggled, but quit when the penknife pricked her.

"All right, you sonuvabitch," he said to me in tones that would freeze a mother's heart, "throw my gun on the bed." He saw me hesitate and jabbed his daughter with the knife point again, hard enough to make her yelp. "I said, throw it, or she gets it!"

I said, "You lousy—".

He sank the knife into her side just below the rib cage and the blood started coming. She screamed and sagged, but he held her up. His bloody knife was poised; a growing stain was brightening her blouse. His voice was the cruelest sound I'd ever heard. "You want me to stick her again?"

I didn't have any choice. I tossed the gun onto the bed. His eyes gleamed hungrily. He shoved Sally away and lunged for it. She fell onto the bed moaning and he came up with the gun in two hands, aimed at my chest, his eyes like hot coals. There was foam on his lips and a red flush to his face. He was so eager his hands were trembling with excitement and anticipation.

Then Mona's gun went off. It was a big gun, carrying .38 slugs, and the one she fired made a black hole in Marshall

Schyler's temple. It was a round, neat mark and looked as if a bug had landed. Coming out was different. It exploded from the other side of his head and brains, blood, hair, flesh and bone spattered all over the wall.

His whole body jumped with the impact and his gun crashed to the carpet before he did. Sally, on the bed, didn't move. She didn't even open her eyes.

As for me, I caught Mona just before she hit the floor in a dead faint.

19

MONA WAS A GUTSY GAL. She came around fast and then did everything I asked without question. First I had her get back into her muumuu, and she zipped it up to her chin like a puritan. I pocketed both guns, left Marshall where he lay and carried Sally down to her bedroom with Mona showing the way. Sally moaned, and she was bleeding more than I liked, but the knife only had an inch-and-a-half blade and she'd been stabbed in a well-muscled region.

Nevertheless, it wasn't something to fool around with and I phoned for an ambulance and had Mona notify the gate with the proper instructions. The room, incidentally, was the one in which Sally had tended me, and now I returned the favor. We cut off her blouse and applied compresses and in between I phoned my lawyer with a quick rundown and had him notify the F.B.I. I told Mona she'd have to undergo a lot of grilling and she should tell the Feds everything she knew. As it turned out, she didn't know much except where Marshall kept his files. The files, however, promised a helluva lot. It took a truck to carry them away.

Sally was examined by medics at the scene. Her wound was viewed as not serious, but she was taken to the hospital for proper examination and dispensation.

I had my session with the F.B.I. agents but went it alone. I wanted my lawyer to sit in on Mona's interrogation so she wouldn't incriminate herself.

Without going into all the boring details, it was a lengthy evening and things didn't quiet down until after eleven o'clock.

Perry Marstan showed up then with the local gendarmerie. The rumors of Marshall's death had reached the force. Perry, hurrying to the fore, eyed the agents unhappily. They were finishing up and he was just coming in.

"What the hell is all this?" he said, dragging me aside. "What're the Feds doing here?"

"It's a drug bust. It's a federal offense."

"Why didn't you call me first? I should have been the one to notify the F.B.I. You should've called *me*!"

"Come off it, Perry, you were in on it."

"What?"

"You were part of the grab. Schyler was paying you. How much?"

He stared at me in shock. "Are you crazy? What the hell's the matter with you, Simon?"

I gave it to him then. "Schyler had a pipeline to the police department. Everything the cops knew, Schyler knew. Everything he wanted the cops to know, they knew." I pointed a finger. "And you were the pipeline."

"How the hell can you say a thing like that?" he blustered. "We had no contact with him. I don't even know the guy."

I shook my head. "The afternoon after Jud Lorne killed Ralph Scorwitch, you cops were looking for Chelsea Powers. You couldn't have known she was a witness unless Jud had told Schyler and he told you. Then when I said

Glenna's killer had fled in a Lincoln, you tried your damnedest to shake my identification. You should have known better, but you had to try because you knew Jud had killed her and you knew it was Schyler's Lincoln he was using.

"Then there was the way you were suspecting me of knowing where Chelsea was. Where was your evidence? Schyler and Jud Lorne thought I knew something because Jud had seen me in her neighborhood. There was no way for you to make the connection unless you had got it from them.

"And who was it who personally tested Jud Lorne's gun and decided there was no proof it had killed Glenna? That was you, Perry."

"But I couldn't match the bullets, Simon, I swear it."

"Then last night, when you had that warrant out for me...? It wasn't a phone number in Manny Floyd's pocket that sent you after me so hot and heavy, it was Schyler telling you I was in on the killings. But he couldn't appear as a witness tying me to the scene so he made you try to hold me on some other kind of evidence. But there wasn't any. That was the tip-off that someone was giving you orders, Perry, your trying to arrest me without evidence. You're smarter than that. So you had to let me go, but you hated to, because you'd been told to jail me."

Perry shook his head. His face was pale and his eyes black buttons. "We've been friends a long time," he said. "I hope you haven't been shooting your mouth off with wild accusations like that to the F.B.I."

I said, "I don't talk unless I can back up what I say. What I'm telling you is only what I got putting two and two together. It's up to the F.B.I. to prove or disprove the answer I get."

"What do you mean, the F.B.I.?"

"I mean they've impounded Marshall's files. The files will tell the story, not I."

"You should've called me first," Perry said reproachfully. "I've got a wife and kids. I had a right to know."

He walked away from me, around a corner into an empty room. There was a key on the inside of the door, but I didn't know it. In fact, I didn't think anything of his walking away until we all heard the shot and found we couldn't get in to where Perry Marstan was until we broke down the door. He was lying on the floor with his service revolver by his side, and what he'd done to his head was what Mona had done to Marshall's. It was another very unpretty sight, and I was the one who would have to tell his wife.

I SAT WITH PERRY'S WIFE until half-past one. The children were asleep and we didn't wake them. I held her hand and didn't know what to say. What do you ever say to a person when someone close has died?

Especially for the wrong reasons?

If it was line of duty, you can talk of God and heavenly reward—at least Father Jack can. It sounds like tin coming out of me.

When it's for shame, and suicide to boot, I don't know if even Father Jack has the words.

I don't.

So the house, when you stopped to notice, was larger than a police captain's salary could afford. So the cars were newer and bigger and there were two instead of one. So Sheila Marstan had the best of line in washer, dryer, refrigerator, dishwasher and vacuum. And all the pipes were copper tubing.

Now she was a widow. You pay for what you get in this world.

I made her take a couple of sleeping tablets at midnight, but it was an hour and a half before she began to get drowsy.

I said good-night and that I'd drop by in the morning. Then I got out of there and back to my own place. I was wondering what the hell I had to hold people's hands for. Perry hadn't been all that good a friend. Some of his cop cronies should have been there on standby, but they wouldn't admit they knew him once it came out that he was in Marshall Schyler's pocket and Marshall was as dead as Perry was. If the check isn't in the mail, you don't buy flowers.

So it was home to the condo at two in the morning, drained and leaden. This had not been one of my good days. That I'd even survived it was thanks to Mona and not to myself. Some tin hero I was. It takes the girls to pull me out of the fire.

The condo had lights going and that was a cheery sight. Chelsea wasn't exactly the type I'd want to tell my troubles to, but she had ways of comforting a man and I needed a little comfort.

Something was wrong with the place, but I didn't spot the trouble until I opened the door and sensed an empty inside. Then I realized the outside was empty, too. Chelsea's rattletrap convertible was gone.

She'd left a note. It was on the kitchen table, held down by a cream pitcher that had left a wet ring. It was written on the back of the note I'd left her, and it said:

Living with you is nothing but sex and TV, mostly TV. I
never see you except in bed. If you want me around,
you'd better find something else to do besides work.
Life is to enjoy, and that's how I'm going to spend
mine. Thanks for the ride, but the road's too short.
                                                    Chelsea
P.S.: If you change your ways, I'll be at Nero's.

I read it twice and sighed. Then I poured myself a drink.
At least she'd left the furniture intact.

At three o'clock the doorbell chimed. It was Sally
Schyler, wrapped to the gills in mink with a gold-threaded
scarf over her head. I said, "You're supposed to be in the
hospital," because I was fresh out of bright conversation
for girls on my doorstep who were supposed to be in the
hospital.

She nodded and came in, smelling of fresh cold air and a
faint perfumed aroma that you wanted to get closer to. "I
wanted out, so they let me out."

"And having no other place to go—"

"Actually, I went home and changed, and spent a little
time getting up my nerve. If I hadn't seen any lights—"

"Nerve? Lights?"

She was close to me now. "I wanted to thank you. You
saved my life."

"I did what?"

"Saved my life. He stabbed me. My own father actually
stabbed me. He would have stabbed me again and again. I
could tell when he did it that he liked it. That was my father!
My own father."

"I'm sure you're misunderstanding."

"Don't apologize for him. I'm not shocked. Honestly I'm

not. Do you know something? I don't know what happened to my mother. All of a sudden she wasn't there anymore. No explanation, no nothing. There were nursemaids. Then there was Mona. But Mona's not a mother, she's like a sister. We feel like sisters. That's why she killed him. Because he stabbed me. And maybe if she hadn't, pretty soon there wouldn't have been any Mona anymore. Like my mother not being there anymore. And it was the same with Carla's mother.

"So don't apologize because he's dead. I'm glad. I never really knew him, but I'm glad all the same. And you saved my life."

I said, "I didn't save your life. Mona did."

She shook her head. "You did. You threw down your gun to make him stop stabbing me. He was going to kill you and you knew it, but you threw down your gun."

"You ought to be in bed," I told her, that being another of my less than scintillating remarks.

"I'm all right," she said. "I really am." She shed her mink over the back of a chair and moved into the kitchen where the light was better. She touched her side and said, "It's sore and stiff, but it really hardly affects me at all." She undid her blouse. "I'll show you."

I didn't tell her not to because I knew she would show me in any event. She undid the whole blouse and pulled it wide. The bandage and tapes were half-hidden by her skirt and she unfastened that next. Up top she wore a see-through bra, and as I've mentioned before, there's a lot to see.

She pushed the skirt down and said, "Oops," when it fell to the floor. Anyway, when she then pulled her pants down a couple of inches, I could view the whole bandage.

"See," she said, "I'm almost as good as new."

I didn't pretend I wasn't supposed to look at everything else. "The rest of you looks even *better* than new."

"That's flattering," she said. "But you've seen Mona and she has a beautiful body. I'm not sure I can compete with her."

"We could always strip you and find out."

"That's right," she said musingly. "If I stripped, then we'd know."

I said, "How about right now?" But she was already ahead of me.

A Special Offer from...

4 Free Mystery Novels!

That's right. You will receive
absolutely free 4 exciting new
mystery novels from RAVEN HOUSE
as your introduction to the
RAVEN HOUSE MYSTERIES subscription plan.

Your FREE books are

Crimes Past
by Mary Challis
The embezzled half million
had disappeared into thin
air. When a corpse turned up
with a switchblade lodged
in its back, it was clear
that one of the thieves had
turned into a murderer!

Red Is for Shrouds
by Mary Ann Taylor
Someone was killing
redheaded girls. Three
of them had been savagely
bludgeoned to death, and
small-town Police Chief
Emil Martin's job was
squarely on the line.

The Crossword Mystery
by Robert B. Gillespie
The queen of American
crossword puzzles was dead.
She'd managed to leave a
cryptogrammic clue to her
murderer, but would it be
found before he killed again?

Murder Takes a Wife
by James A. Howard
He was a professional
murderer with remarkably
inventive methods. He
specialized in wife-killing,
and he was good at it—
very, very good.

**Thrill to these exciting new novels
filled with action, intrigue, suspense and danger.**

RAVEN HOUSE MYSTERIES
are more than ordinary
reading entertainment.

Don't miss this exciting opportunity to read, FREE, some of the very best in crime fiction.
It's a chance you can't afford to let pass by.

As a RAVEN HOUSE subscriber you will receive every month 4 thrilling new mystery novels, all written by authors who know how to keep you in suspense till the very last page.

You may cancel your subscription whenever you wish.
Should you decide to stop your order, just let us know and we'll cancel all further shipments.

CLIP AND MAIL THIS COUPON TODAY!